D1518130

# FOOTLOOSE
# CONROY

# FOOTLOOSE CONROY

•

## Marjorie M. McGinley

*AVALON BOOKS*
NEW YORK

PRINTED IN THE UNITED STATES OF AMERICA
ON ACID-FREE PAPER
BY HADDON CRAFTSMEN, BLOOMSBURG, PENNSYLVANIA

To Mertie, Michael, Douglas, Sharon, and Belinda

## Chapter One

Mike Conroy rode his horse Browny down into the arroyo. The dry gully below him had been washed out many times in the past by a stream of suddenly arriving fast-moving water, and ordinarily a wise man would have avoided it. But he wasn't being wise. *And maybe not much of a man, either,* he thought to himself.

The brown gelding kept his footing and Mike let him half-slide and pick his way down the steep bank as best he could. Nervous, Browny knew that this was something out of the ordinary and he snorted and let Mike know he disapproved of this treatment. The bank was too steep, and Mike should have looked for a gentler slope to go down.

And the brown gelding was right, of course.

Yesterday Mike had quit the Double A Ranch in Texas, which he had been foreman of for thirteen months, with thirty-one dollars in his pocket—all his savings—and his teeth gritted in anger.

He'd ridden straight west.

Defiantly, Mike rode in the arroyo, knowing that the sky

1

in the far distance in front of him held those gray-black heavy-looking clouds signaling rain.

*What the heck is the matter with me anyway?* he thought to himself as he rode.

Once too often he'd listened and believed, as the ranch owner, LuBeth Atkinson, had wooed him with her lies. Then he'd caught her kissing Gerald in the parlor a couple of minutes after lunch yesterday.

"I'll make it up to you," she'd said, running after him, with what he now realized were crocodile tears running down her cheeks.

*Needing me to stay on and be her ranch foreman after her father had died. Using me. Only pretending to care about me.*

He'd gathered his few possessions, saddled up Browny, and left immediately.

What a fool he'd been, he thought bitterly to himself. But no more. He half-hoped Apaches would swoop down on him from the sides of the arroyo and make an end to him.

Apaches were thought to be somewhere up in the Guadaloupe Mountains, to the west of him, right this minute, and there Mike was, riding straight toward them when he could just as well be riding in any other direction.

The bitter truth was, he couldn't blame anyone but himself for his troubles, he thought. Every person within fifty miles of the ranch had expressed their opinion of LuBeth Atkinson; but he'd refused to listen.

*Darn fool!*

And it wouldn't have been so bad if Gerald was a man he respected; or a man that he suspected was a better man than he himself was; but the truth was that Gerald was a shirker: A man who couldn't be depended on to do his work. The other men on the ranch had always had to watch and double-check to see if Gerald had done what he'd been told to do. And Gerald would have been fired instantly if the ranch wasn't as short-handed as it was. The other hands had disliked Gerald and made it clear to Mike that they wanted him gone.

*And, not to my credit, I hadn't listened. What a fool I've been*, he told himself.

As he rode, the cottonwoods that had sprouted, survived, and struggled for life in flash floods were above him on the top edges of both sides of this section of the arroyo.

And here and there in the bottom of the arroyo were the remains of dead cottonwoods that had been uprooted by sudden floods in the past; carried by the water and then dropped as the water receded.

With a quiver, Browny told him that he needed a rest, so Mike jumped down and then slowly walked the horse up a place he saw on the left side of the arroyo where it wasn't so steep.

When he reached the top he walked Browny over to the shade of a larger cottonwood on the level ground. He grabbed a handful of grass and gave her a quick rubdown.

Guilt set in, as the gelding swung his head around and looked him right in the eye as Mike rubbed.

The horse was right. His troubles were not the horse's fault; the horse should not be getting this punishment and the brunt of Mike's anger.

And if Mike got killed, Browny would end up being meat for some Apache's supper. If not today, sometime in the near future when they were hungry. Apaches—on foot—traveled so expertly through their area west of here that they thought of horses more as meat than as something necessary to ride. It made a lot of sense, what with the yuccas, prickly pear cactuses, and the other desert plants scattered about, making it hard for a horse to pick his way around them. No direct path, unless you were on an established trail.

Which Mike wasn't.

"I'm sorry, old boy," he said, patting the horse's glossy brown neck.

Mike took off his hat and poured a little water out of his canteen into his large black hat for the horse to drink. The horse drank, and then he dropped his head and began to nibble a small clump of grass near his feet.

Mike looked around. If it wasn't for the flooding danger, and no year-round water, this would be a pretty, quiet place to live. Here under the glossy-leaved cottonwoods, it was real pretty, and there was some grass here and there. The green leaves on these particular cottonwoods were narrower than the leaves on the ones in Texas, he noticed.

After he let the horse rest awhile, he climbed back up, and they were off again, down in the arroyo. This time he guided his horse down a slope that was not so steep.

He knew one thing. Not where he was going, not what the future might bring, but that he would never fall for LuBeth's lies again. *Or the lies of any other woman,* he thought to himself bitterly.

He kept going over and over it in his head. "I'll make it up to you." That was about as stupid a remark as he could make. You can't "make it up" to a person for a thing like that. She'd been telling him that she loved him for months. *You just don't do a thing like that in the first place, if you love someone.* Couldn't she see that? Where were her brains?

He had to admit that it wasn't her brains that had attracted him in the first place. That was probably his big mistake. Her slim waist and her yellow hair and those pretty, bouncy curls . . . and her full lips. . . . He could still see her inviting lips in his mind . . . and her creamy white skin.

He shook his head to rid himself of the memory.

*No, don't think about that!*

And maybe, he had to admit to himself, that somewhere, deep down, he knew all along that LuBeth was—well, not the most reputable woman in the world. That was why he'd wanted to leave the Double A Ranch after her father's death. But he couldn't bring himself to admit it; not after she said she loved him; said she wanted to marry him right after this year's fall roundup. And he knew that a month ago she'd ordered a fancy white wedding dress to be sent all the way from New York City.

*What a fool I was!*

*What a stupid fool!*

He rode in the long deep arroyo until near dusk, out of sight of Apaches, who, he knew, liked to watch from the mountains and then swoop down on people they saw traveling below. It was incredible how far you could see across these flat plainlike areas from the tops of those mountains to the west of him. He'd been up there once with his uncle.

He found a gentler slope and let his horse take them on up out of the danger of the arroyo flooding as dusk began darkening the sky. Luckily, it got dark fairly late in early July.

He cold camped fifty feet back from the edge, with his ''Improved Henry''—an 1866 model Winchester—and his 1851 Navy model Colt revolver in its dark leather holster laid out right next to him as he lay down and attempted to sleep. Late in the night he heard the rushing roar of water that told him that his guess was correct. An early July thunderstorm, maybe hundreds of miles away, had filled the arroyo suddenly, almost to the top, if he was lucky—and possibly pouring over the sides toward him if he was real unlucky.

He was lucky.

By dawn the water was receding—but not by much yet. He strapped on his gun belt, picked up his rifle, and went to the edge and filled his tin cup, letting the sediment settle before he touched the water to his lips. Then he used the cup to fill up his canteen, slowly letting the dirt settle as much as possible in the cup before pouring it into the canteen.

Better silty, sandy water than none at all. And there was none, or very little, where he was going.

Where, exactly was he going?

His horse drank beside him, as he thought.

In the very early morning light, riding straight toward the Apache stronghold didn't seem as smart an idea as it did last night in the heat of his anger.

And stupid could get you very dead around here. Very quickly.

So what, then?

If east was out—that would be back toward the ranch he'd just left in Texas, and directly west was out, that left north and south.

South? No. No water down there for long stretches. *No.* North? No.

How about northwest, then?

"Northwest," he said aloud to the gelding, as if Browny could understand.

Mike rolled up his blanket tightly, putting his slicker inside it as he rolled, and gathered up the few other things he had scattered about his campsite in careless anger the night before. He stuffed them into a saddlebag, then he brought them over close as he saddled his horse.

He reached down and picked up his blanket roll and tied it down securely behind the saddle.

He adjusted his saddlebags and slid his rifle back into its sheath before he mounted and turned the horse northwest so he could ride around the northernmost section of the Guadaloupe Mountains.

First, though, he would be riding across the Pecos River valley.

Cattlemen driving cattle north from West Texas often followed the Pecos River valley up through New Mexico Territory. The Pecos River valley, he knew, provided both water and grass for the cattle on the journey.

Eventually the cattle would either end up in a railroad car going east or be sold to one of the agents on one of the Indian reservations.

But instead of following the Pecos River north, Mike himself would cross the Pecos and go around the northernmost end of the Guadaloupes and then head southwest down to El Paso, Texas.

Toward El Paso, then, maybe? Maybe. For now, it sounded like the most sensible plan—and a fairly long journey.

He would still be heading into a high area Apaches went back and forth through on their way to Mexico and back, but at least it was north of the Guadaloupe Mountains where the Apaches were supposed to be causing trouble right now.

Apaches who had fled the reservation, as these had, sometimes fled down into Mexico to get away from the U.S. Army that was always, it seemed, after some group or other of them who had run off. Right now, this particular bunch was supposed to be somewhere in the Guadaloupe Mountains directly west of him, which ran down into Mexico.

His choice made, he headed slightly northwest, just after dawn, on Browny. It began as a quiet ride, he and the gelding traveling quietly together on this beautiful, peaceful morning with the large clear blue sky overhead and the cheerful morning calls of birds back and forth to each other.

Were the little birds greeting each other? Saying what a beautiful day it was?

Sometimes there was no other sound but the creak of leather, and the soft thud of the gelding's hooves hitting the yellow dirt here in a pleasant rhythm.

Gradually the landscape was changing to more desertlike conditions, with less grass than on the Texas plains.

Short shrubs here, placed far apart. No trees. Occasional yuccas. Prickly pears. Not much grass here—not enough for grazing cattle unless you had a great deal of land per animal. Occasional arroyos heading directly east-west like the one he'd rode in yesterday because of the rains that came rolling down off the mountains to the west during storms.

A roadrunner dashed comically in front of his horse, it's feathers on it's head raised up in annoyance at Mike's disturbing it. It couldn't make it's dovelike sound because it had a long skinny brownish-gray lizard hanging from both sides of it's narrow beak.

Mike smiled.

''Good boy,'' he said, patting Browny's neck. The horse had not been at all startled by the appearance of the comical bird.

An hour or two later, as the heat intensified, he reached for his neck to grab hold of his old dark blue cotton bandanna to wipe the sweat from his face. It was usually tied very loosely around his neck.

It wasn't there.

Dang! He had broken his own rule about always double-checking around where he'd camped before leaving to see if anything was being left behind. It was too far to go back for it. He knew he hadn't put it in a saddlebag.

With his blue bandanna gone, it meant he was out of a napkin, wash rag, towel, dust protector, sunburn shield for the back of his neck, potholder, foodholder, temporary money holder, and sometime container for small items he didn't want to lose. Dang!

He rode on, annoyed at himself again.

It was hot already!

He rode on.

A little later, he came upon a ten- or twelve-foot-high ridge on the generally flat area and he stopped to take a look around before going over it, dismounting and pushing his black hat back so it was hanging down his back by the chin strap.

He crept up behind the ridge slowly and carefully, being careful not to make an outline or profile of himself.

The ridge here was sprinkled with yuccas, prickly pear, and a few other plants, and the view was breathtakingly huge—and empty—for a long distance, swooping out down below him and out beyond, a big area dotted only with short vegetation here and there growing in the dirt and dust. It looked almost like a giant, very shallow bowl laid out before him.

Beautiful mountains rose sharply up out of the land to the west. No foothills. Two extremes. Flat and then sharp mountain peaks. The Guadaloupe Mountains didn't run north-south, but more southeast to northwest.

It looked quiet and peaceful for a very long distance ahead, out there on the flat bottom part of the shallow bowl.

But that didn't mean it was. Not by a long shot. He looked, for a long time, for any faint trail of white powdery dust or any signs of movement—even tiny specklike movements far away on the other side of the area. After a long while, he was satisfied.

Apaches would have a long clear view for an incredible number of miles from up in those mountains. Almost beyond comprehension, if they'd managed to acquire a spyglass.

He walked back down, put his hat back on, remounted, and rode up and over the ridge and down into the bowl-like area.

He was relieved and glad when he reached the other side of that exposed, flat area and came to the slightly hillier area of mesquite and grama grass on the other side.

As they went over and down the first big rise at the end of the bowl-like area, the gelding decided to relieve himself. The thought crossed Mike's mind that if he was an Apache, he would have gotten down and covered it up so as to leave no trace of his passing.

He didn't.

Chewing a bit of jerky for a while, he rode throughout most of the rest of the morning, the cool of the night giving way quickly to the heat of the day as the sun rose. In fact, the morning coolness had changed rapidly to blistering heat as the sun rose higher in the July sky. He was sweating. He took a drink out of the canteen. He was making good time. He had come a long way, he thought.

There was no place as quiet as the desert, he thought. Quieter than an empty church.

As the heat grew he was careful to avoid the shady side of any mesquite where rattlers might be shading themselves from the sun. No sense asking for trouble.

From a distance, the presence of trees told him he was reaching water—the Pecos River.

When he reached the Pecos, he was forced to ride north

to get to a crossing. In some areas the river's banks were too steep for Browny to go down.

Ah, here was one.

He crossed the Pecos. Once he was on the other side, he stopped to take a drink and let Browny drink and cool off, filling his own canteen. He washed up and let the water cool and refresh him.

He stayed by the river for fifteen or twenty minutes, under the cottonwoods, resting himself and Browny, enjoying the shade.

When he was ready to leave, he mounted up, turned Browny away from the river, and rode off.

His blue bandanna was not there to help keep the sun off his neck. He pushed his hat back down over the back of his neck the best he could. The sun was hitting most of the right side of his back and neck as it rose behind him, climbing up in the east gradually into in the seemingly endless bright, deep blue sky above his head.

Yesterday's treatment of his horse was something that Mike was not proud of. The brown gelding was good at cow work: roping, cutting out, holding herd, and riding the circle. In addition, Browny was a good rope pony. He was smart, not headstrong, like Mike himself.

He dry camped at dusk, watered Browny using his black hat, and slept. He set out early the next morning, covering a lot of miles.

Late morning, he came upon an area of beautiful canyons. He rode around them, following a faint—maybe an animal trail—that he guessed led right around them.

He was right; it did.

He was getting mighty hungry.

Just before noon he came upon a small ranch, down in a wide grassy meadow, with a small stream running through it, edged by cottonwoods. There was a small new-looking plank ranch house closest to him, a corral near the cottonwoods, and a couple of small new outbuildings, which he saw included a small bunkhouse, a tiny saddlery, and a primitive ranch blacksmithy set back a little from the house, in a small wide-doored shed.

A very old wagon, weathered to a pale gray color, was parked near the door of the house.

He intended riding around the ranch when he came over the rise and saw it was there, but a small figure outside of the corral waved to him as if to encourage him to ride down into the flat area below him where the ranch was located.

At first, Mike thought that whoever had waved at him was awaiting someone else's arrival, and had mistaken him for that person, but as he rode closer, he could see that the ranch owner—if that's who he was—was not much more than a kid.

A short-legged but sturdy-looking saddled-up sorrel was in the pole corral near where the kid was standing. The horse was crowhopping and bucking wildly around, close to the poles of the corral on the opposite side from where the kid was standing.

The well-cared-for corral was partly shaded by the cottonwood trees nearby.

The horse looked as if it had just been ridden. It was sweaty, and so was the boy, who had a smudge of dirt on the right side of his cheek.

Fresh dirt kicked up showed recent activity in the corral.

The boy had straight brown hair, large brown eyes, a straight nose, a dark tan, and a real friendly grin on a friendly-looking face. He was about five feet five.

"Hey, you know anything about flea-bitten, no-good, crowhopping horses?" the kid said. "Ole Buck and a Half—that's what I call her, Buck and a Half—that's what she cost—she and I don't 'xactly see eye to eye. That is, except when we're both on the ground—fainted dead away from fightin' against one another," he said jokingly.

The boy grinned again, and Mike found it hard to refuse. The kid was making a joke. Calling a horse "a ten-dollar mustang" meant that that horse wasn't much good. A horse that was worth only a buck and a half, therefore. . . .

He looked at the boy again; he was just a skinny young kid. Seventeen, eighteen, maybe? No. Probably not eighteen yet. Maybe barely seventeen.

"I just call her Bucky for short," the young kid added, still jokingly.

Mike dismounted and tied his own horse to the outside of the corral.

The kid came over and put out his hand toward him.

"Jedediah Jones," he said, "Jed for short."

Mike shook the kid's hand.

"Mike Conroy," he said back. "You really pay a whole buck and a half for *that?*" he said jokingly, nodding toward the horse.

"Yep. Worth every penny, too," Jed said, grinning. "Suspicious circumstances, though. Mr. Webster, over in Cottonwood, Texas, seemed *mighty, mighty* eager to get rid of her.

"Seriously, she's sturdy-looking, don't ya think? Headstrong, though. So far, she's been outsmarting me and winning the 'who's the boss?' fight, hands down. Lets me saddle her, though."

He shook his head in despair as if admitting that this horse was too much for him.

"Want to give it one more try while I'm watching?" Mike said, noting for the first time that the sorrel *was* easy-gaited. She might make a good horse if she learned some manners. And the boy was right, she was sturdy-looking. Mike had already noticed that.

And a crowhopping horse, in his own experience, was only half-trying to get rid of the rider. Crowhopping was stiff-legged bucking. Maybe the kid could do it. It would be good experience.

Jed reached back and pulled on his battered dark brown hat, which had been hanging by the chin strap around his neck down his back, and walked over and pulled himself up onto the sorrel.

The sorrel took off bucking and crowhopping and in less than a minute Jed was thrown to the ground. He got up quickly, brushing and rubbing the dirt off his knees and his trousers with his hands and his hat as he came back over to Mike.

"What part of the north you from, Jedediah?" Mike asked.

The kid grinned.

"Now how'd you know I was from up north?"

"A cowboy from up north *rises up* in his stirrups—don't sit down—when he rides a buckin' horse. Like you just did. A cowboy from down here doesn't . . . he bobs up and down in the saddle, sittin'."

"*Did* move here from the north—Fort Laramie—with my . . . my Dad when I was seven," Jed admitted. "Learned to ride from my father."

The kid had hesitated a bit before he said "my Dad," as if there was something the kid had thought of and then purposely left out.

Mike climbed over the fence—no use opening it and taking a chance on getting run down by "Bucky." He looked at Bucky, sizing up the horse's personality, as she stood inside the corral.

"At least she's not a roller," Jed said, hopefully.

Mike nodded his agreement. A bucking horse that tried

to roll every time you mounted was the worst, as far as Mike was concerned.

Without being told, Jed showed Mike that he had good manners by walking over, untying Mike's gelding, and moving the horse out of the sun and the flies and picketing him in the shade of a cottonwood tree over to the right of the corral.

Then Jed walked back over and brought the brown gelding some water that was in a dented tin bucket near the corral. Finally, Jed walked back to the corral.

Mike watched as the kid did all this, all the while still studying Bucky.

The kid seemed like a nice polite kid, but his eyes looked a little sad.

Bucky was nervously watching both of them. She had calmed down somewhat during the short break, but her eyes were still rolling, showing the whites, and she was still acting skittishly, throwing back her head, tossing her mane, and stamping her feet.

Jed leaned his arms over the top pole of the corral and watched both Mike and Bucky to see what was going to happen next.

Once in a while Bucky looked around the corral as if looking for a place or a way to escape from Mike.

Taking his time, Mike slowly walked over to Bucky and let Bucky smell him, talking to Bucky and stroking her neck.

Patiently waiting, letting Bucky take a good look at him, waiting until Bucky settled down.

Mike waited until Bucky's eyes showed only brown again.

Finally, after about ten more minutes of talking and stroking, Mike swung up and sat on the horse, and both balanced and braced himself—ready—as Bucky began her trip counterclockwise around the corral, hopping and bucking.

Once Bucky fell, on purpose, with a loud grunt, but she gave enough warning that Mike realized what was happening and got his feet out of the stirrups and was able to jump off without getting his leg bones stove in.

"That won't work, girl," Mike said firmly, and he got right back up on Bucky without taking time to brush himself off.

Bucky was not that bad. It took a while for Mike to give the horse "some proper manners," and make Bucky act more polite and willing to have a rider on her back and follow simple directions. Bucky was, all in all, not a real dangerous critter. She'd just needed a few "kinks" taken out.

At the end, Bucky was circling the corral not in a docile way, but as if she finally agreed, somewhat reluctantly, to tolerate a man on her back.

She'd still need some work learning to follow the neck-rein signals, Mike thought. She'd need someone to teach her to follow the directions of the rider using the reins— practice with a patient rider on her back. She needed a rider who she could trust to be the boss, consistent and firm.

Mike said all that to Jed.

"Thanks, Mr. Conroy," Jed said, in a heartfelt way. He shook his head. "I was gettin' to believe that this mare's head was plumb air—empty—south of her ears. We been buttin' heads somethin' fierce for days.

"I'd be obliged if you would come to the house and have some coffee and a bite to eat with me after I water Bucky."

Mike nodded his agreement to the kid.

"That sounds like a good idea," he said.

But if the kid had this much trouble with Bucky, how was he going to succeed ranching here by himself?

Was he by himself? Mike had no way of knowing. It didn't seem polite—or, indeed, any of his business to ask. He didn't want to insult the kid.

Maybe his Ma and Pa were just gone for the day. He quietly looked around as Jed gave Bucky a drink of water, then followed Jed to the small ranch house. There was a small clothesline in back of the ranch house, but it had only what looked like the boy's clothing hanging from it.

Inside, Jed put some fresh water into a coffeepot, added coffee, and set it on the stove. There was already the remnants of a fire going in the stove, and Jed threw some more small pieces of firewood inside that he found as he moved about the small kitchen area.

Wood for fires was one of the things, like water, that was usually precious and scarce around here.

The place looked cared for. If the kid was alone, he was doing a good job caring for the place. An old worn-out broom leaned against the wall closest to the door.

Mike noticed that there was very little dirt and dust on the plank floor. That took a lot of work in a place where dirt being tracked inside was a constant problem. Maybe the floor had even been swept just this morning.

The kid was a worker.

Jed ladled water from a bucket inside the door and offered Mike a drink, holding the ladle out toward him.

Mike drank and then Jed drank. The kid was again being polite and mannerly, letting Mike drink first.

"Thanks," Mike said. " 'Preciate that."

The kid nodded.

Mike wanted to warn him about being so open and friendly to strangers, so he said, as he stood near the door and looked around, still seeing no evidence of anyone living there but the kid, "Looks like you are alone out here.

Aren't you worried about it . . . bein' so close to where Apaches are supposed to be holed up right now?''

The kid walked over and checked to see how the coffee was doing on the stove, then got two battered tin cups off a shelf off to the side of the little stove. He stopped, then, holding the two cups in his hand and turned and looked at Mike, with a look of embarrassment.

The kid didn't answer yes or no directly, but said, ''Truth be told, I was awful glad to see it was *you* ridin' up . . . glad to see a familiar face.''

Mike was silent, while he tried to figure out what the kid meant. Familiar face? He didn't remember ever having seen this kid before. And the kid must have *very* good eyesight if he recognized him—who he was—while he was still up on the ridge overlooking the ranch. . . .

Jed put the cups on the table and then looked at him.

''You used to throw us kids red-and-white-striped peppermints—all wrapped in paper—when you rode through town over in Blue Quail Run—in Texas—when I was a kid. You probably don't remember me.''

''You were one of those little kids?''

''I was the kid, well, I was the one . . . well, I kind of had a fat face back then.''

A picture formed in his mind of a kid with a chubby face and straight brown hair and brown eyes in the group of kids he used to throw candy to when he worked on the Bar SW Ranch outside of Blue Quail Run about six years ago. It was shortly after the war had ended—his first job after the war ended, in fact. He remembered hearing some story . . . something about the kid, but couldn't quite recall what it was. . . .

''That was you?'' he asked, surprised.

''Yep. Every time you came into town you'd buy some penny candy and throw it to us kids. It was a big treat.

You were our hero. Say, why did you do that? The other cowpokes would already be in the saloon drinkin' up their wages.''

''I don't know. I guess 'cause my Uncle Marcus used to do that when I was a kid and I liked it. Sort of passin' the tradition on.''

''What happened to your uncle?''

''Horse shied unexpectedly. His head hit a rock.'' His Uncle Marcus was the last surviving member of his family—except for himself. Now his uncle was confined to bed, confused and disoriented most days. A woman, Mrs. Fisher, who was his nurse as well as his housekeeper, watched after him in a small house in Austin.

''Never was right after that.''

''That's too bad.''

He nodded. It was three years ago that the accident happened. He still felt bad about it sometimes, and he didn't want to talk about it further.

The kid sensed this and didn't ask. He busied himself, instead, reheating some beans and bacon and pouring the coffee, when it was made, into the two tin cups he had placed on the rough plank table.

The kid motioned for him to sit.

He walked around and sat on the bench on the opposite side of the table from where the kid was standing.

The coffee was good.

After getting them each a plate, fork, and spoon, which were surprisingly clean, the boy sat down across from him and ate hungrily.

Mike did the same, suddenly realizing that he hadn't eaten much since yesterday noon. The portions were generous.

After he drank the coffee and ate, he went outside with Jed.

"Let me fill up your canteen," the kid said, "before you leave." Before Mike could say, "I'll do it," Jed left, hurried over to the cottonwoods, got Mike's horse, and walked the brown back over to Mike.

"Thanks," Mike said. While Mike was saying this, Jed took the large canteen off the horse, filled it from the bucket inside the door, and put the canteen back where he'd gotten it.

"What do I owe you?" the boy asked.

"Nothin'," Mike said. "Maybe someday *you* throw some penny candy to some kids," he said, grinning, as he swung back up onto his horse, his saddle creaking as his weight settled on it.

"I want to pay you," Jed said, "I got money . . . or a fancy silver belt buckle my father left me, that I could give you, for doing me this favor. He died a few months back. Left me this. . . ." The kid swung his arms, indicating the ranch.

Mike nodded, then he said, "Looks like a nice place. Hope you do well on it, Jedediah. But be *careful*. You *sure* you don't want to leave here for a while and go to a bigger settlement 'til the 'Paches settle down again?"

"No. This here's my home," Jed said firmly. "And I want to pay you," he said again.

Mike picked up the reins and mounted.

"No need," he said. "Just be careful from now on. Keep a rifle and maybe a handgun handy when you're out working around the ranch. And keep a good eye out. Apaches are not that far from here, if my news is correct . . . and sometimes troublemakers can come through. . . ."

"I know," the kid nodded, "and drifters, or outlaws who are no good, or rustlers. I'll be careful. My Pa tole me that already before he died of the fever. Thanks for your help,'' the kid said.

''My pleasure, Jedediah,'' Mike said, as he tipped his hat and rode off.

## Chapter Two

He looked back once just before he rode out of sight, and the boy was still watching him and waving. Now that Mike was at the top of the crest, Jed had taken off his hat and was waving that. He hadn't gone back to work.

The kid was probably very lonely.

He hoped Jed would be all right out here alone. Jed shouldn't have mentioned to Mike that he had money. Mike should have told him that, but he didn't think of it quickly enough.

But maybe the kid had the right idea. Cattle wandering the breathtakingly beautiful land here and multiplying, a house, an ax, a knife, a little silverware, a gun, seeds, a hoe, a coffeepot, a frying pan, a wagon, and a horse or mule.

Maybe he himself should settle down somewhere, after the Apache thing quieted down, raise a few head of cattle. A small ranch with a year-round source of water, enough grass . . . You only needed about thirty head to start.

It was not a bad life, was it?

Nah, footloose he was, and footloose he probably would always be, he guessed, no different than the thousands of other ex-soldiers from both sides of the conflict who were wandering around the west since the war ended.

*An' in the war we all got used to shooting each other in a way my gentle little Ma would not have approved of,* he thought.

Some men he had come across out west here were run-nin' away from memories of the war, or some bad deed back East.

Others, like himself, were too restless—no longer able to just go back home and live with peaceable folk any-more—to live an ordinary life. *An' not about to take any guff from anyone anymore.*

A cowboy soon learned not to ask too many questions about the past of the man working next to him. For one thing, you might find out that he had been on a different side of the war. . . .

And yep, now that he thought some on it, ranch life—in Texas or here in New Mexico Territory—an' bein' a lone, wanderin' cowpoke—suited him just fine.

LuBeth had almost caught him and tied him down. Maybe he was lucky he found out in time, rather than find-ing out after they were married that LuBeth was fickle. That's what she was, fickle. And Gerald . . . well, maybe they deserved each other. Neither one could be trusted.

His thoughts were interrupted as he heard another rider coming up from behind. He turned and he saw Jake Her-man, one of the cowhands from LuBeth's ranch.

''What are you doing here?'' he asked, surprised, as Jake rode up to him and pulled in his reins about eight feet away.

''Had a meetin' in the bunkhouse after you left. We all decided that in this partic'lar case, our loyalty was to you and not to the Double A brand. We all pulled up stakes about an hour or two after you did. Left LuBeth and Gerald all alone on the ranch,'' Jake said, chuckling at the memory. ''Gerald's a no-account loafer, that's what he is. She made him foreman after you left. Ain't none of us would work for him. Not even for five dang minutes. When we *all* left at once, we left them in a fine pickle,'' Jake said, no longer smiling. ''Deserve every second of it, too.''

Jake paused for a moment, thinking back over what he had just said. ''Yep, our loyalty, as I said, was only to *you*,'' he said soberly, nodding his head slowly.

''You all left on account of me?'' Mike said, surprised and moved. It was an unusual thing that the ranch hands had done, as most cowboys were loyal to the brand.

''Yep. 'Spect that a few of the hands are following even now, on your trail, tryin' to catch up to you, see where you're goin' . . . where you're foreman next—what you're doin' next, same as I am. 'Course, none of 'em are as good trackers as me, so I had to leave a clear trail for 'em,'' Jake said, jokingly.

''Heard outside of El Paso, there's a ranch, the Circle T, that's lookin' for a new foreman. Thought that's where you might be headed.'' Jake looked around and ahead of them, nodding his head as if pleased with his own guess as to Mike's direction.

Tall and lean in the saddle, Jake had a few more years on him than Mike did. His brown hair had a few gray hairs beginning to make streaks through it, and his pleasant-looking, good-natured face was weathered, the result of many years out in the sun and wind. When he smiled, as he often did, there were deep wrinkles near his eyes.

Mike had mixed feelings as he looked at Jake. It was nice what Jake and the others had done, and very loyal, but what would he do with a bunch of out-of-work cowpokes?

He didn't even have a job himself, or know for sure where he was going. If they followed after him, he'd feel responsible for them. He felt responsible for them *now*. He, of all people, who wanted to be footloose, now had to worry about other cowboys besides himself.

Secretly, he hoped that no one else besides Jake had followed him.

Jake didn't seem to be sharing Mike's worries.

Grinning, Jake said, "So, where are we going, Boss? Are we going around and down to El Paso?"

He was letting Mike know that he'd noticed, tracking him, that Mike was headed slightly northwest, and that he knew that to get to El Paso you could go around the north end of the Guadaloupe Mountains and then on down southwest to El Paso. Jake's well-kept shiny black gelding pranced underneath him sideways a bit as if to say that he was ready to get moving again.

"Darned if I know," Mike said, as he urged his horse forward. "That's the first I heard of a job near El Paso."

He had had no way of knowing, up 'til a couple of days ago, that he would even be *looking* for work.

"Lead on, then," Jake said. " 'Darned if I know' sounds like a great place to me. Is that north, south, east, or west of here?" Jake added, jokingly.

"Northwest, then southwest, I guess," Mike said, letting Jake know that his guess was right. He couldn't help smiling at Jake's good-naturedness as they set off, with Jake riding companionably alongside him. Jake, after all, was in the same boat as he himself was now. Footloose.

And he appeared to be taking it well.

"What y'all been doin' since you left the ranch?" Jake said. "Surprised I caught up to you so fast."

"Stopped to uncork a horse at a small ranch," Mike said,

explaining in a few words that he had taken the rough edges off a bronc.

"Ya git 'm unroostered?" Jake said, conversationally.

"A mite," Mike said. "Wasn't too bad. Mare."

A couple of hours later, Mike again had mixed feelings when he and Jake were joined by Wade Sanderson and Bobby McKearney.

Wade was Mike's age, about twenty-seven, and was short, but very muscular, with sandy-colored hair and dark blue eyes.

Bobby was nineteen, and had shiny but unruly long black curly hair that he had trouble keeping under his hat. Sometimes a curl or two fell out and got in his face, and he had a habit of sweeping his hat off and then replacing it on his head, to try to readjust his hair, especially when he was nervous. He was trying to grow a large handlebar moustache like Wild Bill Hickok's, but so far it was mighty sparse.

Thin, he was a few inches taller than Wade, and he sometimes complained that his back hurt him if he spent too many hours in the saddle.

Mike's own hair was black, and he had blue eyes.

The one other year-round cowboy on LuBeth's ranch, Carl Glover, who was also the cook, had decided to go home for a visit. His parents lived near Houston, and he was on his way there now.

Bobby McKearney had brought coffee, a couple of pots, sugar, beans, beef jerky, and hardtack with him, being the only one both cool-tempered and sensible enough to stop in town for supplies before heading after Mike.

As they rode, they traded news about what had happened to each of them since they left LuBeth's ranch.

The four of them rode together companionably, and

about three o'clock Jake said, "There's an area of canyons up ahead. Beautiful country."

About a half-hour before dusk, they camped by a small spring near some boulders. They made their small fire where the cottonwood trees and the surrounding yellow boulders would hide the smoke from the small fire from any Apache eyes. Bobby put coffee on to boil.

Because it was a low spot, the spring had bubbled to the surface in this area.

First thing, Jake, Mike, and Wade paid Bobby back for their share of the food.

It was then that Bobby got the nickname "Cookie," after announcing that he would be the one who did the cooking for the group from now on.

Jake had begun teasingly calling him Cookie as they ate. It was the name usually given to the camp cook on a cattle drive north or on a roundup.

Mike, Wade, and Bobby knew by that that Jake was relieved—and covering up that fact by teasing—that Cookie had been smart enough to think of supplies for them all. In effect, the name Cookie was partly joking and partly an admission of admiration, by Jake, that Cookie had been smart.

Bobby's gentle-looking eyes lit up when he was called Cookie, accepting the new name as a compliment.

"Coffee's ready," Cookie said a few minutes later.

Cookie poured coffee into the tin cups that the other men held out and then filled one for himself out of the coffee-pot and set it on the ground beside him to cool.

Then, knowing better than to ask if any of the men had seen any Apaches—because everyone knew without mentioning it that it was the Apaches that you didn't see—the ones sneaking up on you or watching you—that you had to worry about—Cookie asked instead, as he stirred the beans and passed out the hardtack, ''Did the kid at that ranch you stopped at have any news about them 'Paches that was causin' trouble near here?''

Mike shook his head no, as he eased himself into a more comfortable position on the ground. ''He knew less about it than I did. He didn't even seem to be aware they were so close,'' he added.

He stopped talking then, because he'd started trying to chew some of the hardtack. He decided that he'd hold up on eating any more of the hardtack until he could crush it among the beans that Cookie was warming, rather than risk breaking his teeth on it. He took a swallow of coffee to help get the hardtack down. It wasn't easy. But at least it didn't have insects in it like the hardtack did back in the war.

''Those 'Paches could be anywhere—from Ojo Caliente to deep into Mexico,'' Wade Sanderson said as he poured himself a cup of coffee. Ojo Caliente meant Warm Springs in Spanish.

''Yeah, but most likely, the last I heard for sure in town was that they was holed up somewhere in the Guadaloupe Mountains,'' Cookie said.

His information matched closely the information that Mike himself had gotten, so he nodded his agreement.

''That's what I heard,'' Mike said. ''I was worried about that kid, being alone out there.'' He was still worried. The kid didn't seem to take his warning seriously enough.

The others nodded.

''What was that kid's name?'' Cookie said, stirring the beans he was heating up. ''Was it Jeremiah, or something? I heard that there was a kid who was left a ranch in that area—kid that was a half-breed. Mother was Sioux Indian. Died of typhoid or somethin' like that, didn't she, when the kid was five? Can't rightly recall. . . . Kid and his father came down here from the north after that. From Fort Laramie, or someplace, wasn't it? I ferget the details. Used to know the details, but I ferget.''

Jake said soberly, ''I thought I heard somewhere that the kid's mother was murdered when she was left on their ranch alone. Husband and kid had gone to town for supplies or something. Came south and lived for a while near Blue Quail Run, in Texas after that, I recollect.''

''Jedediah Jones,'' Mike said. ''This kid's name was Jedediah Jones.''

So that was what the kid had hesitated about, that pause before he had said ''my Dad.''

He had sensed that there was something that the kid was omitting. He felt very sorry for the boy if the second story was true. Some people didn't like Indians and considered them fair game to kill if they were found alone on a ranch like that. He could imagine how the boy felt when he arrived home with his father and found her.

''I hope we don't run acrost any 'Paches,'' Cookie said, changing the subject. ''They roast yer head, I heard.''

There was no need to say more. They had all heard enough horror stories of torture. In Texas, they'd had to deal with Comanches.

Wade shuddered. ''What I seen in the war was bad enough. I hope I never have to come acrost anything like that done by no 'Paches.''

But they did, and it was not something done by Apaches, either, Mike found out.

## Chapter Three

Midmorning, Browny snorted, and alerted Mike that something was in the area to the left of the sloping area where they were riding. Already on edge and alert, the group had been watching vultures circling, gradually convening on an area ahead of them—to their left—for ten minutes. Had the Apaches killed someone over there?

As they rode, they'd seen the large, ugly, powerful birds swooping around in arcs high up in the air, large blackish-brown wings angled slightly upward as they soared, then circling and gliding down silently, rarely flapping until they disappeared out of sight as they landed.

Mike lost count of them. He pulled up, just about the same time as Jake did, next to him.

"Go and see?" Jake inquired of him, meaning he himself, Jake, would go.

"I'll go, too." Mike said, and he reined the gelding to the left of their trail.

Jake nodded and they rode off.

Once, in the War of the Rebellion, Mike had seen a

man—caught stealing from the tent of a wounded soldier—
being punished. The thief had been caught red-handed.

Mike himself had not taken part in the punishment, but
the thief was stripped naked to the waist by an angry crowd,
his head was shaved, and a big sign was hung around his
neck which said in very large crude black letters

> THIEF
> THIS MAN WAS
> CAUGHT
> STEALING FROM A
> WOUNDED
> FELLOW SOLDIER

The man was drummed out of the unit in disgrace: two
young boys, Robert Dunning and Edwin Cobb, who were
about fourteen or fifteen at the time, and who were the
drummers for Mike's unit, beat a somber rhythm on their
drums as an enraged group of Mike's fellow soldiers brutally hit and beat on the man. Drummed out of his group
of fellow soldiers and former friends forever.

But this was worse.

As he and Jake came in sight of what the vultures were
waiting for, they could see a man tied, saddleless, on a
bridled dapple-gray horse. The man's head was crudely
shaven, with nicks and cuts all over his head.

A big sign hanging by a rope around his neck said THIEF
in large letters.

The man was brutally sunburned. There was no telling
how many days he had been tied to the dapple-gray horse
without water. The horse was weak and in a state of terror, its
eyes rolling at seeing the ugly red-headed vultures circling

and boldly landing nearby, or flapping their wings loudly and with the man tied on his back.

The gray whinnied and stamped his feet in a fruitless attempt to drive off the vultures.

Jake slid down silently off his horse, a small, horrible gasp escaping involuntarily from his lips.

Jake was stunned. So it was Mike who first went toward the horse, talking softly: ''Whoa, there, honey, it's just us come to help.'' Then, ''Jake, get that man down quick,'' he said as Jake dismounted and rushed to help, being careful not to spook the horse worse than it was.

''I don't know how long I can hold 'er,'' Mike said, as he slid his hand quietly toward the bridle to grab it.

Jake had his knife out in seconds, and began to cut the man free. He had to reach under the horse's belly to cut the thick ropes that tied the man's legs to the horse.

The man slid down, unconscious, into Jake's arms. Mike had never seen anything like it. The man was cooked by the sun. It was the worst thing Mike had ever seen.

Some emotion reached out from that man to himself, something that was unexplainable.

It was the strong gut feeling that this man was not a thief. Something about this man told him that. Or something in the man's face, reaching out to him. It was a face of innocence. A face with no sign of hardness or treachery. A face of suffering.

The large, red-headed turkey vultures, discouraged by Jake and Mike's arrival, flapped heavily off, struggling as usual to get their large dark bodies off the ground and into flight.

Mike let the horse go, putting the reins down on the ground in front of the horse after moving the horse about ten feet away. Many horses were trained to stand still when the reins were put like that. This horse did, so Mike returned and knelt next to Jake who was still holding the man in his arms.

The others, Wade and Cookie, came over the rise seconds later, too curious to wait back where they were.

"Oh, God," Cookie said. " 'Paches?"

"No. White Eyes," Jake said sarcastically, using the derogatory name Apaches called white men. Jake pointed to the sign.

"White men did that?" Wade said, unbelievingly.

"This isn't an Apache's *style*," Jake said, again sarcastically, pointing to the sign.

"Help me get him out of the sun," Mike said to them, and Cookie and Wade dismounted rapidly.

Jake took off his own hat and put it on the man's head, and Wade went for the gray blanket he had rolled up with his slicker behind his saddle.

Mike gently cut the sign from around the man's neck and threw it on the ground.

Underneath the sign was the only place that wasn't severely sunburned on the man's body. It had left a white rectangle on his chest.

They rolled the man up loosely in the gray blanket.

Jake took his canteen down off his horse and, opening it, gently forced the lip of the canteen in between the man's lips and let some water dribble into his mouth.

"Not too much all at once," Wade said, and Jake answered tensely, "I know that, fool."

"Sorry," Wade said.

"What are we going to do?" Wade said.

"Get him to some shade and try to help," Mike answered, as he saw Jake, Wade, and Cookie looking at him, waiting for him to tell them what to do.

"It's out of our way, but Thunderbird Canyon is the closest place I know of," Jake said.

Their heads bobbed in agreement. Thunderbird Canyon had one thing going for it over all the other places that they could choose to go. No Indians ever went there.

Indians believed that the Thunderbird stole Indian babies. Sometimes large birds of prey—some of which had traditionally followed buffalo herds to feed on the sick or dying left behind—especially during the summer rainy season—were sometimes seen by Indians carrying what appeared to be large objects in their mouths. When Indian babies disappeared, it was natural to assume that the birds had carried them off.

It was a legend. Mike had no idea if it was true. But the Indians believed it. That much he knew.

Thunderbird Canyon was rumored to be a nesting area for large birds of prey. As far as Mike could figure out, the Thunderbird of this legend was not an eagle. Eagles just wintered in New Mexico Territory, they didn't nest there. So that left eagles out. He wondered if thunderbirds were some kind of unusual large condor.

"How are we going to get the man there?" Wade asked. "There is no wood around here to make a litter."

When Mike began to try to lift the man toward his own saddle, Wade and Cookie realized what he planned to do, and hurried over to helped him get the unconscious man up on Mike's horse, in front of Mike, so that Mike could keep him in the saddle.

They rode off, Jake leading the way, and leading the dapple-gray horse, and then Wade and Cookie, and then Mike and the unconscious man last. The man was wrapped as loosely as he could be in the blanket, with Jake's hat set gently on his head. Mike sat behind the man, holding him in the saddle.

They headed north toward Thunderbird Canyon, following Jake, who appeared to know where it was.

About every hour, they stopped and Mike gave the man water again, although Mike began to doubt that it was doing any good. The man seemed too far gone.

Near dusk, they reached the entrance to Thunderbird Canyon, and rode up the narrow, seldom used trail and into the canyon. Here, antelope gathered at dusk, and Wade managed to get off a good shot at one. They would have fresh meat for supper. Wade rode off to take care of the antelope.

Dusk came early here because of the steep canyon walls. Rimrock surrounded them on all sides, except for the grassy canyon floor. A few cottonwoods and oaks were by the spring in the canyon.

Mike reined the gelding in near the spring, which was a quarter of a mile further into the canyon from where the antelope was shot.

It was located in the middle of the canyon floor, in the lowest place.

Looking up, Mike was very aware that there was only one way out of this canyon.

Jake and Cookie came over to help Mike get the man down, and then Cookie went to the stream to get water for the man.

As they were riding, he'd felt the heat of the man's body, even through the loose blanket. He had a high fever. A couple of times the man moaned in pain as they went over a bumpy stretch, and he thought to himself that that was a good sign; the man might be regaining consciousness. Although that might, in fact, be bad because if he was conscious, he would be feeling more pain.

Wade arrived at the spring with big chunks of antelope meat wrapped in a cloth, which he gave to Cookie as soon as he dismounted. Then Wade went to the spring to wash the blood off himself, and hurried back quickly to help.

Mike and Jake carried the moaning man and laid him gently down on the blanket which Wade laid out by the spring, under a large oak tree.

Wade took off his white silk bandanna, wet it at the spring, and began sponging the man off as best he could. When he was through, he gently dried the man off and then put a second blanket—Mike's—over the top of the man. Now they could clearly see that the man had been beaten as well as what else had been done to him; bruises and cuts and scrapes were all over him.

No one spoke, each silently taking in the horror of what had been done to this man.

Because of their silence, as the last bit of light disappeared, off in the distance, under the trees, Mike saw a grayish brown rabbit hop out, unaware that his usual dusk eating place had been invaded. The rabbit looked for a moment at the strange scene, and then hopped away, silently disappearing into the grassy undergrowth.

Wade took sponging the man off as his job, trying to get the fever down.

Mostly, Jake and Mike stood helplessly by, watching, and then Jake, with a doubtful shake of his head, went to help Cookie by cutting up the chunks of antelope into steaks for supper.

It was clear he didn't want to hang around and watch the man suffer. Usually a thoughtful, gentle man, it was clear, by the way his knife hacked at the antelope meat and the tight look around his mouth, that he was angry.

Cookie looked over at Mike, raising his eyebrows to show his surprise at Jake's uncharacteristic anger, then set about building a fire to cook the meat.

Wade still sat to the left of the man and tended him as best he could.

A while later, they ate in almost total silence. No one seemed to have much of an appetite.

They didn't want to disturb the man, and no one had anything to say. Jake, Cookie, and Mike sat silently around the small fire, each one glancing over from time to time at the man, not quite knowing what to do.

Wade stayed next to the burned man, sitting on a corner of the blanket.

The man, cooled off from his earlier spongings by Wade, began to shiver after it got dark. His jaw shook, and his body couldn't seem to stop shivering.

He moaned a few times and said ''Uhhh'' a few times. Wade leaned over each time to check him and adjust the blanket.

''At least the fever has broke,'' Wade said hopefully, tucking the blanket more closely around the man.

Jake shook his head in silence, his face lit by the fire-light. He was indicating that he didn't think the man had a chance.

Mike himself intend to agree with Jake. The man didn't look good.

Jake and Cookie fell off to sleep as they saw that Mike and Wade intended to both stay awake and care for the man and keep watch.

Every so often during the night Mike gave the man a drink of water, and he and Wade tried to get him to drink a bit of water with jerky stirred into it that Cookie had made into kind of a soup, but the water was all the man could seem to let them dribble in his mouth.

In between, Mike and Wade tended the fire because the man was still cold and shivering.

Mike had a feeling that the man once had been good-looking. He had nice even features, from what Mike could tell—it was hard to know, with all the blisters and burned areas, and the lack of hair, all but gone except for facial stubble which had grown on the days the man was on the horse.

Finally, almost at dawn, the man's eyes fluttered open.

Mike got close, leaning over the man as close as he dared, for it seemed that the man was trying to speak.

Wade was near Mike, on the other side of the man, listening.

It seemed that the man was trying to tell him something that he felt was very important.

"Not . . . not . . . a thief," the man said, finally, getting it out only slowly and painfully.

"I know," Mike said. "I know." He felt a terrible swell of emotion rise in himself.

Then Mike said, "Can you tell me why they did this to you?"

"Don't know. Water?" the man said, "Wa . . . water on my father's land? Killed my father," he managed painfully to say. "Said it was *suicide* . . . father shot three times." His voice broke when he said suicide.

"They said it was a suicide, when he was shot *three* times?" Mike asked.

The man managed to nod, barely. He added slowly, with great effort, "In the back."

"Who are these people?"

"Nat Pierce and his men. . . ." That was all the man could manage before he fell back to sleep or into unconsciousness.

Mike felt, rather than heard, a movement at his side, and he turned and saw it was Jake, awake, beside him, listening.

"I heard," Jake said. "I couldn't sleep."

"I think he's dead," Jake said a minute later, after looking at the man.

He was.

## Chapter Four

They buried the unknown man. Then the four men gathered rocks silently and piled them about a foot and a half high over his grave so coyotes couldn't come and dig the man back up.

It was a few hours after dawn when they laid the last yellow limestone chunk of rock over the buried man.

"What now?" Wade said.

Cookie said, *"Take off yer hats."*

They did, and Cookie said a few words he obviously knew by heart from the Bible.

Mike thought Cookie was through, and almost put his hat back on when Cookie surprised them all by adding, almost in a scolding voice: "Psalm 32. 'I will instruct you, says the Lord, and guide you along the best pathway for yer life; I will advise you and watch yer progress. Don't be like a senseless horse or mule that has to have a bit in its mouth to keep it in line. . . . *Many sorrows come to the wicked,* but abiding love surrounds those who are good and decent and trust in the Lord.' An' Lord, we trust you to

39

watch over this here poor man for all eternity, and to *punish* them what did this. Amen.''

Looking at Cookie kind of suspiciously as they walked away from the grave, Wade said, ''Cookie, did you all make that up about the bit in the mouth of a mule? I don't remember my Momma's Bible talkin' about no stubborn horses and mules.''

Cookie stopped and looked Wade right in the eye. ''Ain't yer Momma never *taught* you nothin' about the Good Book? An' didn't I tell you it was Psalm 32? Go look it up if you don't believe me!''

Wade shut up, chastised. Cookie was not one to lie about something.

In fact, he had done pretty well, and he'd made his voice sound like a real pastor, Mike thought.

Ever since Cookie had gotten his new name, he'd been acting different! This was a whole new forceful side of Cookie he'd never seen before. Cookie was usually so mild.

When Cookie was through looking Wade in the eye, he walked back to the grave and pounded a rough cross he had somehow made out of two rough bits of wood he had scrounged up from somewhere, into the earth at the head of the grave.

The other three waited at a respectful distance until Cookie rejoined them.

''You can all go down to the ranch near El Paso and wait for me,'' Mike said quietly as the four men walked soberly back under the trees to where the already saddled horses stood.

''I'll be along soon; apply for that foreman's job when I get there. Should only be a few days behind you.''

''What are you going to do?'' Cookie said.

Mike could tell that Jake and Wade already knew what he was going to do, by the reluctant looks on their faces.

"Mike, yer not . . ." Jake said.

"He is, look at his face," Wade said.

"Mike, it ain't yer business," Jake said. "You don't even know the man. An' the sign said that he was a thief."

"You don't know that," Mike said. "Just because the sign said it, don't make it the truth."

"But . . . El Paso," Jake said.

Mike thought for a moment. He was torn. He did feel responsibility for these men getting work soon. But to ride away and leave this . . . to just act as if it hadn't happened . . . to let the men who had done this terrible thing just get away with it . . . how could he live with that the rest of his life?

"He tole me that he didn't do it; he didn't steal—that someone wanted his father's land and shot his father three times," Mike said. "I believe him."

"An' did this to the son to get rid of him?" Wade said, seeming to be the one most eager to think the man innocent. ". . . so's they could have the ranch . . . the land?"

Jake reluctantly nodded that he had heard the man say this.

"But we don't even know the man's name," Jake said, even then seeming to know that he was losing this battle.

"Doesn't change anything."

"Mike, *yer* a cussed stubborn mule," Jake said.

As they had already broke camp and packed up everything, and filled their canteens before burying the dead man, Jake swung up onto his horse.

Wade and Cookie followed his example, doing the same.

Only Mike stayed on the ground.

It was quiet for a few seconds, and then they heard the sudden loud flap of a large bird's wings directly over their heads, unseen, above the live oaks that grew in this strange canyon.

Cookie involuntarily jumped a bit, startled, and said, "This place is scary. Let's get out of here. I'm ready to skedaddle, vamoose, and just plain get the heck out of here!"

Wade nodded. "I agree with *him!*" he said, looking up through the leaves above him in the oak tree they stood under. They all looked up but could see nothing but leaves and sky peeking through.

Mike looked at them, nodded agreement, and mounted. He didn't like it here, either. He felt sorry that the man would have to spend eternity alone here, but it couldn't be helped in this heat.

"I'll see you all in El Paso, then, in a few days," Mike said.

"The heck you will," Jake said. "You may be a stubborn fool, but I'm stickin' with you."

"That goes for me, too." Wade said.

"Me, too," Cookie said.

They turned their horses and rode toward the mouth of the box canyon, following their own tracks, back the way they had come in.

Mike rode first, followed by Jake, leading the man's dapple-gray horse, and Wade and Cookie trailed behind.

"You got a plan in mind, Boss?" Jake asked, once, as the trail grew wide enough for him to momentarily ride alongside Mike.

"I was planning on going back to where we found the man, and then backtrack his trail. When we get close to a town or ranch, we can do two things: one, let that horse behind you go, and follow it home, or go to the nearest town and see what's what, first. Mebbee both."

Jake looked around at the high rimrocks above them and said thoughtfully, "We could picket the man's horse outside of town if we want to, until we look around both places, ranch and town. What was the guy's name that the man said did it?''

''Nat Pierce.''

They arrived at the mouth of the canyon and rode on outside. Mike was relieved. From a closed-in canyon area to a view that took your breath away with its beauty. An immense, flat, seemingly empty space stretched out in front of them, dotted only with desert plants—mostly yuccas— here and there.

Mike breathed a sigh of relief. The Indians were right about that canyon . . . there was something mysterious, about it. Maybe it was the odd shadows cast by the high rimrock that shut off the sun, morning and afternoon, he guessed, on both sides. Sunlight only in the middle . . .

Most of the journey into New Mexico Territory—so far—the land had been breathtakingly beautiful, Mike thought.

And it wasn't that this canyon wasn't beautiful . . .

They were facing a ride now through an area that was dry. Rain probably had not fallen here on the night that it had filled the arroyo near where he had camped that night. Thoughts of LuBeth filled his mind. It was too bad that Arthur Atkinson, LuBeth's father, had died in December. He was a good man. LuBeth . . .

He forced himself to think of something else. Soon, there would be more July thunderstorms, what his Uncle Marcus had jokingly called the ''monsoon season.''

His Uncle Marcus had been a great world traveler before Mike's parents had died and his uncle had come home to care for him. Before that, his uncle had sailed to the Caribbean, and to England, and to many other places, using money that he had been left by Mike's grandparents. His Uncle Marcus had been to Africa and China and India. India was where his uncle had learned about monsoons.

He'd given up his one great love—traveling—to come home and care for Mike.

Now Mike was paying him back, in a way, sending most of his wages every month to the housekeeper-nurse to pay for the expenses of the old man and his nurse.

His uncle had been a good man, and tried his best to raise Mike as best he could. His uncle's philosophy was "If you have *tried* to do something and you fail at it, you have still lived a better life than if you had tried to do nothing at all."

His own father had used his inheritance money to move the family from Ohio, and to buy land along the Mississippi River, land which had suddenly disappeared one day when the river decided to permanently change course.

What land was left of their property after the river's change of course was barely enough to survive on. Soon, they had lost that, and then cholera had swept through one summer. . . .

He was jolted out of his thoughts as his gelding's front left hoof made a rock roll off suddenly to the side.

He had better pay attention to what was going on now, and not let his thoughts wander.

He only hoped that the trail they were going to follow, once they got back to where they had found the man, would not cross any of the cattle trails going through here.

If they crossed the trail of large cattle drives, they'd have to depend solely on the dead man's horse's knowing his way home, for the tracks would be lost among hundreds or thousands of others.

How far away had the man come from?

Probably at least two days, judging by the man's condition. Could he have lasted much longer than that in this heat?

There had been stories of people lasting many days in

the desert, but with clothing on, and not in the man's condition. And he had been viciously beaten, and probably kicked, before his ride began.

Maybe three days at the most?

Three days of intense suffering.

They reached the area where they had found the man. By now the full force of the afternoon heat was shimmering off the scrubby desertlike area in front of them, making mirages of wavering water.

There were no trees here in which to take noon shelter out of the sun, so they kept on riding.

Mike kept tracking.

The tracks were leading them northwest now. There were places that the horse had stopped, and places where the horse had aimlessly wandered.

They dry camped for the night, and were off the next morning.

By mid-morning, they reached a place where the tracks veered off to the left, and by that time Mike realized that he knew where the nearest settlement was. It was Aguardiente, a place he was familiar with.

They stopped to talk over what to do next.

Although he'd never come to Aguardiente from this direction, it was a place he knew. He said that. Aguardiente was about three or four miles away.

"I'd like to be the one who backtracks and scouts around the place where this trail leads," Wade said forcefully. "When I see a ranch, or see where the tracks have led, I'll come back here and follow the trail behind you into Aguardiente."

Mike started to argue, but a look on Jake's face said to Mike "Let him go. It is important to him."

Wade added quietly, "Mike, I want to."

Reluctantly, Mike agreed. "Be careful," he said, frowning.

He was not at all sure that this was a good idea. But Wade was his own boss now. He wasn't working for Mike now, he was an equal partner in the journey.

Wade turned his horse to the left, and Mike, Jake, and Cookie watched him ride off, backtracking the lone horse's tracks.

Mike could change part of his plans now. He didn't need to picket the dapple-gray horse that the dead man had been riding outside of town somewhere. If they were heading to Aguardiente, it was safe to take the horse there. He told that to Jake and Cookie.

For he knew Aguardiente well.

## Chapter Five

It was mid-afternoon when they reached the small trading post called Aguardiente by the local people—the Spanish name for a fiery liquor.

Originally it meant a specific brandy from El Paso, but now it meant any strong liquor. It was made from the agave plant, the same as tequila. Aguardiente was a drink which had been popular with mountain men in Taos and Santa Fe since the 1820's, and was pronounced ah-gwar-DYEN-tay.

It had a reputation for making a man want the attention of the opposite sex; which sometimes brought trouble out here where women were usually as scarce as legs on a rattlesnake.

A new wooden building, which Mike could see now was a livery stable, had been added since Mike was here last, to the south of the original trading post building.

Aguardiente was run by a man known only as Toothpick, for obvious reasons, once you laid eyes on him.

Toothpick came to the door of the one storey adobe building, as he always did, to see who had ridden up. He always stood a little bit back from the doorway, Mike knew, with a Sharps rifle ready, just inside to the right of the door, propped up against the wall, ready for use.

He usually had a toothpick hanging out of one side of his mouth or the other. He was tall and spare, but with a powerful frame and very thick black hair. He had friendly dark gray eyes that could turn to match the color of the cold iron of the barrel of the Sharps breechloader in a flash.

Today he had a mild, agreeable expression on his face.

"Hey, Mike," he said in greeting, his eyes dismissing Mike once he had recognized him and studying Cookie and Jake instead, sizing them up.

The mild expression remained on his face, and Mike knew that Jake and Cookie had passed the examination.

Although few other people knew it—and might make trouble if they did—only a few people besides Mike knew that Toothpick's mother had been an ex-slave from Louisiana.

Very light-skinned, and said to be very beautiful, she and Toothpick's white father had come west to settle over in the central Texas area before the war. There they were unknown, and she had successfully passed as white the rest of her life. Toothpick's father had been a blanket and long-underwear salesman from Illinois whose territory was throughout the south. That was how they'd met.

Toothpick considered that no one else's business. A quiet man, Toothpick stood straight and strong and few had the courage to question him when he spoke.

Mocho was the single exception to this, and she was able to henpeck him with impunity whenever she felt like it.

Toothpick would never be rude to a woman, Mike knew, and in particular to a tiny one like his wife Mocho. She was barely five feet tall.

His skin was an odd shade of tan that nobody in this

area questioned. Toothpick spent most of his time indoors in the adobe building, a combination saloon/restaurant/trading post.

His wife—part Indian and part Mexican—remained out of sight for the most part. Her name was Mocho, which meant "mutilated" in Spanish.

Cowboys used the term *mocho* to mean a cow with either a cut-off tail, a droopy ear caused by damage from ticks, or one with a droopy, misshapen horn.

There was no outward sign of mutilation on Mocho, although she always wore her hair covering her ears. And, in fact, her arms, face, and neck were the only part of her Mike had ever seen not modestly covered by clothing.

She seemed to bear her name proudly.

Toothpick came outside. Today Mocho pushed out from behind him and came forward, outside, into the sunlight, to see him better. She shielded her eyes with her left hand, blocking the sun as she came to the edge of the sidewalk outside of the adobe building.

"Mike," she said, in her friendly way, smiling at him.

Her long, black, shiny hair fell forward over her shoulders, ending up lying on her ample bosom.

"Hello, Mike," Mocho said again, stepping just off the rough planks that ran across the front of the adobe building and into the dirt of the street near Mike. "Been too long. Glad to see you."

"Same to you," Mike said, smiling back at Mocho. Her colorful red-and-yellow Mexican-style short-sleeved dress hung down to just above her ankles after being belted by a black, red, and yellow thick-woven belt at her waist. Below that, Apache-style high deerskin boots peeked out from under her skirts.

Toothpick walked over to where Mike sat on his horse

and in a friendly way tied Mike's horse to the hitching rail for Mike, before Mike swung down out of the saddle.

Toothpick was too polite to ask, but Mike knew he was wondering why Mike was here now.

"Tell you what a fool I been," Mike said jokingly to Toothpick, but softly enough and to the side as he dismounted, so that no one else could hear.

He and Toothpick waited until Cookie and Jake went inside with Mocho.

Standing in front of Jake's horse and his own, but coming around to the other side of the hitching post onto the plank porch to talk, Mike stood near Toothpick and in a quiet voice, he told of the fool that he'd been at LuBeth's ranch and what had happened since, leaving out for now the part about helping the kid with the crowhopping horse and the burned man.

When Mike finished, Toothpick grinned and slapped Mike on the back. "I got what you need to fix you right up," he grinned. "Come on inside."

Inside, Jake and Cookie were standing at the section of counter in the store that was considered the saloon area.

Straight back from the door there was a counter with a passage way to the back rooms in it. That section was considered the trading-post area.

A few tables and chairs were in the far left of the room, and it was an area where Mike had played cards with Toothpick a few times in the past, betting dried beans instead of money, because they were both poor at the time.

As he passed Jake and Cookie, Mike said, "Go easy on that stuff. It'll addle yer brain." He directed the statement to Cookie, who was young. Jake, he knew, could take care of himself.

He walked over and sat at a table in the front left corner with his back to the wall. He was worried about Wade. He hoped Wade was not being foolhardy, and was being careful. He was relieved when he saw from this new vantage point, that Jake and Cookie were only drinking regular whiskey and not *aguardiente.*

For safety reasons, none of the tables were placed directly in front of a window. The table Mike was at was in the far left corner and another was behind the front wall between the door and the window. The third table was by itself further back along the corner near the back left wall, and was the one that Mocho usually sat women at.

In fact, few women had ever been in here in the building besides Mocho during the times Mike had been here previously.

The right side of the room was set up as a small store or trading post, but it was different than the typical general store.

General stores usually had their groceries on the right, dry goods on the left, and hardware items in the back. Aguardiente was different.

At Aguardiente, Toothpick's adobe had the saloon-restaurant on the left and the complete general store on the right as you came in the door. It consisted of the counter, which was filled with items, and the shelves which were filled with merchandise, along the right side of the room. It was a small area.

As a result, the trading post/store carried only the necessities. To many men, that meant food, tobacco, ammunition, and liquor.

Today, Mike could see that Toothpick had added a lot of new items and more wooden shelves to the right since the last time Mike had been here. The shelves were piled so high with merchandise that the merchandise reached to the bottom of the next shelf and was crammed in.

Mike guessed that Toothpick did a good business. And

as it was apparent that business was thriving, Mike realized that Toothpick and Mocho might be beginning to be vulnerable to robbers and thieves. They were a long way from nowhere out here by themselves and off the beaten track.

Although they tried not to show it, it was apparent that since he had last visited, Mocho and Toothpick were no longer leading a threadbare existence.

Toothpick came over and sat down next to him, and leaned back comfortably in the chair.

"You run the livery stable, too?" Mike asked.

Toothpick said, "Nope. A man from Missouri arrived a few months ago. Had a rough time of it in the war. Lost an arm. He runs it. Man goes by the name of Ted Buchanan. Short for Theodore. Before the war he ran longhorns from Texas back home to Sedalia, Missouri.

"Don't know how he manages with one arm but he does. Guess he's used to it. Uses the stump to hold things under his armpit with. Then uses the other arm to do the work; shovelin' out the stalls an' all, an' you only need one arm to shovel out oats or corn if you got a good scoop."

Mike nodded. "I got to get the horses out of the sun, then I've got something else—very important—to talk to you about."

Toothpick rolled the toothpick in his mouth from the left to the right side. "I ain't goin' nowheres," he said, still leaning back in his chair.

"I'll be back in a minute, then," Mike said.

He went outside and brought the four horses over to the livery stable.

Inside, he introduced himself to the man Toothpick had said was Ted Buchanan.

Ted Buchanan was a large man with a ruddy face and unruly looking reddish-yellow hair which he wore long and parted in the middle. Mike had the feeling that the yellowish-looking hair was red hair that was starting to turn gray. He had a fierce look to his heavy eyebrows which Mike suspected covered up a compassionate and generous nature, as he saw how the man took the reins of each of the horses, one at a time with his good arm, and led them gently to stalls he had prepared.

The horses went right along as if knowing the man was a good one, and that a generous portion of oats and water were waiting for them in the stall.

The man had a way with horses.

"Horse lover, are ya," Mike said, trying to start conversation.

"Yep. Had my fill of mules when I was in Missouri," Ted said genially. "Treat a horse good, he usually treats you the same back."

He added, "That ain't always so with a mule. Horse *wants* a man for a friend; tell him what to do. Not so with a mule."

If he'd been over the Santa Fe Trail back and forth to Missouri many times, Mike knew Ted must be a competent livestock handler.

"Toothpick said you'd run cattle back to Missouri," Mike said.

"Run my share, and then some."

Mike noticed the empty left sleeve of Ted's shirt was not folded back and sewed to the upper arm as Mike had seen done by a lot of men who'd lost an arm in the war. Instead, the sleeve of the brown shirt was cut off below the stump and sewn closed neatly. He wondered who had sewn it. Toothpick hadn't mentioned a wife.

"Tooth tell you about his book?" Ted asked.

"No. I just got here." In fact, Mike felt a moment of shame, as this question had made him realize that he had not asked Toothpick how he was; only selfishly barged ahead telling Toothpick his own problems—and—not even telling him *all* his problems yet—he hadn't told Toothpick about the sunburned man and Nat Pierce.

"Tooth' wrote a book. Sent it back east to New Yawk City. Book of yarns and fairy tales fer kids. Publisher's gonna publish it in a coupla months," Ted said.

"Toothpick is a man of many surprises," Mike said. "Admire that very much. Good man, too."

"He'll do," Ted agreed, and Mike got the impression that that was a thing that Ted Buchanan didn't often say about another man.

The last of the four horses was now in its stall.

"You want me to pay now?" Mike asked.

"Nah, pay when you leave," Ted said. "Plenty of time to worry about that later," he said, indicating that he trusted Mike.

"Thanks," Mike said.

The horses were obviously being well seen to by Ted, so Mike walked back to the adobe building.

A large wagon was parked outside. Someone had come to buy supplies while Mike was gone.

Back inside, Toothpick was gone from where he'd been sitting at the table with Mike, so Mike decided he'd walk back over to the same table and sit down and wait. Jake and Cookie were still standing over at the saloon area drinking, standing in the exact same places they had been when Mike left.

Also inside, Mike saw a large rowdy looking man with a full head of dark reddish-brown hair and a full, wiry beard sitting with two ladies about the man's age at the table in the back far left.

He guessed they were all in their mid-thirties, he thought as he walked.

Mike was surprised a little to see the women there. Mike

guessed that the man was good-looking underneath his beard; at least in the two ladies' view, the way they were both paying close attention to him, and fussing over everything he said.

Mike did have to admit that the man had a commanding presence. He looked as if he was a man who wouldn't take orders from anyone. He looked to be well over two hundred pounds. Maybe two-hundred-twenty. Muscles. Barrel-chested.

Mike had reached the table and he sat down quietly in the same chair that he had been in before when talking to Toothpick. It was near the front corner, his back to the wall, and he could look out over the whole room, the same as before.

To his left now, toward the back, was the table with the two ladies, alone at this minute because the large man had risen and was walking over to the saloon area, probably to buy a drink.

Mocho was in the back room preparing the three of them something to eat, Mike guessed, and Toothpick was probably filling an order the new people had placed in the trading post part of the store.

The two ladies left alone at the table had cups in front of them, with coffee or tea in them, Mike didn't know which.

Because the room was small, Mike could hear clearly when the thinner woman said to the chubbier woman, "Mabel, what's Rusty's favorite food?"

The chubbier woman looked at the woman who had spoken a long time before she answered. Then she said, "Chicken."

"Chicken? Chicken, Mabel?"

Mabel said firmly, "Chicken."

Shortly after that, the thinner woman, a short yellow-haired woman, got up and left the table to go and talk to Mocho, who had come out of the back room.

Mabel was a chubby, busty woman with curly brown hair and a few scattered freckles over her nose, wearing a brown dress. She looked over at Mike with just the slightest beginnings of a satisfied smile on her full, red lips. She was pleasant-looking.

Leaning over toward Mike confidentially, as if revealing an important secret, she said, "That woman who just left is Alice Fickerby. She's been after my husband, Rusty, for months—ever since she and her brother moved onto the ranch next to ours."

She indicated the large red-haired, bearded man who had left her table and was now over by the saloon area by raising her chin toward him before she sipped out of her cup; the man she had called her husband Rusty was standing near Jake and drinking whiskey from a small glass. She looked over at Rusty fondly.

"Actually, my husband *hates* chicken," she said.

"But I thought you said . . ." Mike said.

The woman smiled.

Mocho had evidently concluded her business with Alice Fickerby.

Mocho came over with a bottle of whiskey and a glass. She put both on the table in front of Mike and said, "Toothpick says this is on the house. He's busy now but will be over to talk to you as soon as he finishes loading an order into the wagon outside."

She smiled shyly.

Mike smiled back and poured himself a drink, as Mocho left, and watched as Alice and Rusty both returned to join Mabel at the table. Soon Mocho returned with three bowls of beef stew and cornbread for the two women and the man.

Then she returned with three more bowls and cornbread

for Mike's table. Jake and Cookie came to join him and the three men ate with gusto.

During a lull in the conversation at his own table, Mike heard Alice say to Rusty, "Come to dinner at my ranch Sunday night, Rusty. I've bought twenty chickens from Mocho. I'll be serving *chicken* Sunday night and a *lot* of nights after that. Come over whenever you feel like having chicken."

Rusty looked surprised by the unexpected invitation, but he caught himself quickly, and mumbled something about his ranch and that he would be too busy.

Mabel looked over at Mike as if to say, "See, I told you so."

Mike grinned back, and Mabel smiled at him and then turned away, back to paying attention to what she was eating.

When Rusty, Mabel, and Alice Fickerby were done eating, Rusty paid Mocho for their food and for Mabel and Rusty's supplies with double eagle gold coins, each of which was worth twenty dollars, Mike noticed.

Shortly after that, Mabel, Rusty, and Alice left.

The three of them walked outside to the wagon, which Toothpick had already loaded.

A minute went by, and Mike saw the wagon pulling away, passing the front window packed high with supplies, going north, complete with the noise of twenty unhappy white squawking chickens in wooden cages on the wagon bed.

Mike smiled as he saw the chickens going by the window. Alice would have a tough time stealing Rusty away from Mabel. Mabel was more than a worthy opponent.

Shortly after that, Toothpick joined them at their table and the three men told Toothpick how they had found the burned man on the trail, and about what had happened to him. They told him where Wade was, and how they had come to be at Aguardiente.

Each time Mocho approached, the men stopped talking so as to spare her hearing about what had happened to the man.

Cookie said, ''Mr. Toothpick, you should have seen what that poor soul looked like . . . all burnt up so bad by the sun an' all.''

They stopped as Mocho brought Toothpick a bowl of stew and cornbread.

After she left, when they got to the part about Wade wanting to backtrack the trail, Jake surprised Mike by saying that he figured that Wade wanted to do it because Wade's own brother had died in a fire in their barn in Kansas when Wade was a kid. When Wade saw how badly the man was burned, even though it was sunburn and not by fire, it had struck a chord with Wade and he wanted to help.

Mike could still vividly picture the man's terrible-looking face, and how Wade had so gently sponged the man off.

He had seen his share of burns in his time during the war, and he could understand how Wade had felt.

But when they got around to mentioning the man's name that the burned man had said had done it—Nat Pierce—Toothpick's expression changed. It was as if a shadow passed over his face.

''Bad hombre,'' Toothpick said, clearly worried. ''Best steer clear of him and his bunch if you can.''

''Don't know as I can,'' Mike said, then he added, ''Don't know if I can steer clear and let a man get away with a terrible thing like that in all good conscience.''

## Chapter Six

"That throws a new iron into the fire," Toothpick said. He meant Nat Pierce, Mike thought to himself.

"In here once, and buffaloed a jasper, for no reason," Toothpick said. He meant that Pierce grabbed a man's handgun away from him and knocked him unconscious with it.

"There was no call for him to do that," Toothpick said. "Pierce is just vicious," he added.

"Is he a killer?" Cookie asked.

"Yep. Restless, short fuse. Unpredictable. The *worst* kind. Won't think about somethin' a split second before he goes and does somethin' crazy," Toothpick said. He thought a minute and then he continued, talking slowly and looking intently at Mike.

"Best steer clear, Mike. You can't help. People tend to *disappear* when they cross Nathaniel Pierce. *Friends* of Nat Pierce's enemies disappear, too." He looked pointedly at Mike and then at Jake and Cookie.

"Once, a man disappeared goin' from here to home, an'

59

all he had done was shot off a tiny piece of one of Nat's cousin's pinky fingers in a *fair* fight. Shoots first, thinks about it later—if then. Nat's cousin—Billy Joe Pierce— was cheatin' at cards.

Some say Nat was a spy in the war. Personally I don't believe it. Likes to puff his feathers up; make people to think he was more important than he was in the war. Has a nickname around here,'' Toothpick said, leaning forward and whispering, and looking around the room as if to make sure no one else but themselves could hear. ''Behind his back, people call him D.B.E.''

He paused and looked around again.

''That's short for Despised By Everybody. More of a back-shooter than a man likely to git you in a fair fight. An' likely to pick you off with a rifle from a distance . . . the man would never face you in a fair fight.''

''Do you know who the burnt dead man might be?'' Mike asked.

''Not for sure. So many men have disappeared around here lately. Vanished, you might say—that it's hard to tell for sure.

You might ride around the ranches 'round here, see who is missing. Plague of robberies, horse thievin' and rustlin' goin' on lately, too. There's some dang big empty spaces 'tween lawmen around here. And Nat Pierce knows the law is far away.''

''Seems to me he's takin' advantage of that fact,'' Jake said.

They all knew that each region had a federal marshal, but U.S. marshals dealt only with federal crimes.

Next, in the states and in the territories, each county had its own sheriff.

And last, every town had it's own local marshal—the lowest paying, most thankless job. Most places the local marshal had to clean the streets of litter, lock up drunks, and shoot stray dogs as part of their job.

And the truth was, there was no town here. Just the store, and now the livery stable. Perhaps, some day, this might be a real town.

Maybe someday New Mexico would even be a real state, not just a territory.

But not today.

That left the county sheriff as their only local lawman.

Toothpick said, ''Bryce Rushford and his son Jim raise mostly sheep and a coupla hogs. Think your description closest fits them two men, father and son. You might want to check their place first.

''If it's them what's dead, yer in luck. Bryce Rushford is the *county sheriff's brother.* That should cause the darned sheriff to finally get his lazy butt over here and do something, fer *once,* about what's been happenin' 'round here!''

He paused, and then added, ''I'll send someone to get him over here, anyways, soon's I finish here with you. Even if we have to go over there ourselves and drag him here.''

The men at the table all nodded.

Everyone was talked out. It was silent at the table.

It was time to leave.

Mike pushed back his chair and got up. Jake and Cookie did the same, and then Toothpick got up and they followed Mike to the counter on the store side of the room.

Toothpick went around to the back of the counter, and each man paid for their meal.

After Mike paid, he spotted a neatly folded pile of bandannas on the counter, and he picked out one that looked identical to the blue one he had lost. He removed it from the stack and placed it on the counter, at the same time reaching in his shirt pocket for money to pay for it.

Toothpick surprised Mike by waving his money away and handing the blue bandanna to Mike.

"Thanks, Toothpick," Mike said.

"Think nothing of it," Toothpick said. "It's a gift."

"Guess we'll take a ride out to the 'baa and oink' ranch," Jake said to Mike, as Jake picked out and paid for a new black hat. He was referring to the pig and sheep farm that Toothpick had mentioned. The Bryce and Jim Rushford place. The most likely place.

Even though Jake had made a joke of it, it was a brave thing to say, seeing what Toothpick had said about Pierce killing any friends of those who went up against him.

Mike appreciated it.

"Thanks, Jake."

He thought a bit.

"On the other hand, it might be better if one person went out there and scouted around first."

Cookie and Toothpick shook their heads in agreement.

"Three riders raise more dust," Cookie said. "More likely to get spotted." It was a good point.

"You don't think they'd have the nerve to just blatantly take over the Rushford ranch, do you?" Jake asked.

Toothpick shook his head and motioned with his hand, indicating that he didn't know. He walked out from behind the counter and they followed him outside to a few feet away from the hitching post in front of the adobe and looked in the direction that he pointed. North.

"There's a faint trail you can follow. Goes to Bryce Rushford's place ten miles out. The two of 'em live . . . or lived alone out there. Water's all right there, but I wouldn't say it was nothin' that you should git kilt over, though. Otherwise, the description could fit the Rushfords. Could be them."

"What about Wade?" Jake asked. "Shouldn't we wait for him?"

"Fact is, I was beginnin' to worry a bit about Wade," Mike admitted. "He should've been here by now."

Jake said, "I think maybe Cookie should wait here for Wade, and you and I should go together to the Rushford place."

"We got the horse the burnt man was riding in the livery stable," Mike said to Toothpick. "Think you could tell whose it was by lookin' at the horse? There was no saddle on it, but . . ."

Toothpick didn't reply, but silently walked over to and inside the livery stable behind Mike. Jake and Cookie followed behind as Mike led Toothpick over to the stall where the dapple-gray horse was.

Behind him, Mike heard Cookie ask Jake, "How far away *is* Sheriff Rushford?" and he heard Jake reply " 'bout seventy miles away, in Calabasa, best I can figger out from what Toothpick said."

That was about right, Mike figured.

Ted Buchanan, the livery man, was nowhere in sight.

Toothpick looked carefully at the horse Mike showed him, and at the brand, but he shook his head. The horse was an ordinary dapple-gray, a soft muted dappling, with no particular markings.

"Not sure. Bryce Rushford, the father, bought horses from the Box D Ranch. But so have a lot of us. Sorry."

Jake said, "I changed my mind. How about Mike goes to look at the Rushford place, and I go back and see if I can locate Wade? Cookie can stay here in case Wade shows up."

"Sounds good to me," Mike said, as they both saddled up. Mike left some money with Toothpick to have him pay Ted Buchanan.

Back at the adobe, Mocho filled their canteens and Jake rode off back the way they had come into town, while Mike rode north in the direction that Toothpick had shown him before.

Cookie and Toothpick went inside to wait.

The trail was faint, but fairly decent to follow, as there were ruts from the regular use of a wagon between the Rushford place and Aguardiente for supplies.

He thought as he rode.

Nat Pierce would not be the first person out here in the west who used the excuse of ''punishing thieves or rustlers'' to run off people they didn't want settling, or timid people whose land they wanted, mostly for their water.

He half-expected to ride up and find Nat Pierce and his men on the Rushford ranch, settled in, and willing and ready to fight anyone who wanted them off.

Truth was, there was probably no one, other than Mike himself and his friends who *cared* what had happened to Bryce Rushford and his son Jim, if that was who the dead man was. Well, Toothpick had seemed to care, but he wasn't even sure it was the Rushfords. Maybe it wasn't.

His gelding switched his tail. Mike looked behind him; a large fly was bothering his horse. He took off his hat and waved the fly away as he rode.

Could a large rancher in the area have hired Nat Pierce and his men? Maybe a large rancher wanted the Rushfords gone.

And more than once, people with power had run off ranchers who had been there a long time; and ranchers who had been given Spanish land grants long ago. Some of this land had been taken by fancy—sometimes crooked—legal maneuvers, some by outright force, from the many Spanish and Mexican descendants of people who had settled here long ago.

Sometimes people even did the opposite; tried to use a useless old Spanish land grant to take over a legally titled piece of land. Disputes over land had gone on for centuries here in New Mexico Territory.

But Toothpick would have known if any of this were true in this case. In fact, he had said, more or less, that he didn't think the Rushford place was anything worth fighting over . . . and that, in this area, usually meant water and good grass.

Toothpick had mentioned specifically that he didn't think the Rushfords' water was more than just adequate.

At what he figured was about nine miles from town, Mike stopped just below a ridge to check his guns and rifle.

It was an area of mesquite and bunch grass. Some shale and some ravines, and a rock spur here and there. Not great grassland, like there was further east, where the tail end of the great plains came down into Texas and even into parts of eastern New Mexico.

He usually carried his handgun with one empty chamber for safety. He loaded the sixth chamber in his handgun. Maybe he'd keep that chamber loaded until this thing was over.

He checked to see that the rifle would come out of its sheath easily.

When he was sure his guns and rifle were loaded and set, he rode slowly over the top of the ridge and saw, about a mile away, an adobe ranch house. One lone tree, probably an old oak, stood in back of the house. A couple of other shorter trees stood where Mike figured the spring was.

No telltale dust was stirred up from here down the slope to the house, and no sign of horses or activity in sight.

Mike was tense, anyway. He'd have hidden his horse or horses out of sight if he was Nat Pierce.

He rode slowly forward, tense, ready for anything.

Still, he saw no sign of anything moving. In the distance, he thought he heard some sheep bleating faintly, but he couldn't see sheep.

As he rode up he looked around.

No pigs, either. He could see pigpens made out of cottonwood logs off to the right, built half under the far side of the big oak tree and half out, so that the pigs could go in the shade when it got too hot in the sun. The pigpen fence was down, and the wooden troughs inside were bone dry, not damp, as if water had been in there recently or for a few days, maybe.

He watched for any movement, any shadow that seemed out of place, ready to draw his gun.

One lone scrawny brownish-red chicken walked around the corner of the adobe, ignoring both Mike and his horse, pecking at the dirt.

"Hallo the house," he called loudly, as he rode his horse up close.

There was no answer.

Mike dismounted and swung down. The hen didn't like this and squawked, then hurried off under the oak tree's shade.

The door of the house was open five or six inches.

Walking over, he pushed the door open with one hand, his other hand hovering over his holster.

It appeared to be empty inside. He went in.

At least one chicken had come inside to explore, as there were about a dozen chicken droppings on the floor just inside the door. Some droppings looked old, some newer.

It was neat and tidy inside, but dusty. It looked as if men lived there . . . men's clothing hanging from pegs. No women's things.

But there wouldn't be; Toothpick had said there were just the two of them living here, father and son.

Water bucket inside the door to the right—empty and dry as a desert bone.

Food supplies undisturbed. Not much there.

No dirty dishes on the table.

On a wooden shelf on the wall above the water bucket there was a picture of three people standing together—a pretty woman standing stiffly alongside two men. He took the picture down and looked at it.

It was him! The younger man in the picture was the exact shape and size of the burned man, and Mike *knew* that it was him by the size and shape of the face, the nose, and the width and slant of the shoulders!

The other man was a pleasant-looking, gray-haired older man; it must be a picture of the father. The older man was smiling in the picture.

The man who supposedly committed ''suicide'' with three bullets in him.

He put the picture carefully back on the shelf.

He studied the place.

A sleeping area was blocked off by blue-and-white-checked curtains in the rear of the room. The curtains were pushed back now, out of the way. Two beds were back there, one made up neatly, the other with covers and quilts rumpled up.

There was one pair of well-worn boots near the unmade bed that was at the back left part of the room.

Mike went outside, closing the door behind him.

On the far side of the oak tree, beyond the pigpens, he found a place with muddy footprints of many sheep that led down a slope to the spring.

If he'd owned that spring, he'd have cleaned it out and walled it up, had the sheep drink from an overflow area instead of the actual spring. Would have made it cleaner. Toothpick was right.

About a hundred and fifty yards from that, he found a new grave, up on a slight gravelly slope.

Although there was a pile of rocks on it to keep coyotes out, there was no sign or cross on it.

Son probably didn't even have a chance to make one, Mike thought.

When the son didn't leave after they killed the father, had they come back to get him—too soon for him to even put a cross on his father's grave?

Almost immediately, then, after the ''suicide,'' they'd come back for him? Within a day or so?

He looked around, but found nothing else he thought important.

There was no sign of the pigs. Either they had been let loose or removed. Stolen, and sold or eaten.

He whistled, and his horse came to him.

He mounted up and rode over in the direction that he had heard sheep bleating. It was better over here—grassy all around, he saw, as he rode slowly and cautiously over an eight-foot rise about three hundred feet from the area of the spring and the ranch house. It was a large meadowlike area, and a flat grass-covered area stretched out for quite a distance on the slightly rolling plains in front of him, dotted only by occasional short shrubs and prickly pear.

The large flock was there, guarded by a black-and-white sheepdog. Kind of long-haired for this area—with the heat an' all, Mike thought. Black spot over the right eye, hair hanging down from his neck, like he was part collie.

Mike didn't approach the dog or the flock.

He turned his horse and left, riding past the empty house again, and then toward Aguardiente, thinking.

One ''suicide'' and one man labeled a thief. One deserted ranch. Bryce Rushford, the father, was the ''suicide,'' and Jim Rushford, his son, was the ''thief.'' Son was neat; had made the father's bed, possibly, after his death. Or the father had made it the morning of his death.

The other bed unmade, the boots left by the bed. Jim Rushford, the son, was rousted out of bed in the night? A surprise attack? The attackers knew that Jim had no need for boots—they *already knew* that he was going to be killed.

Whoever it was was not interested in sheep.

That was a brave dog. Who knows what the poor thing had had to eat? How many days had the dog gone without food?

Dang! He thought to himself, and turning his horse once more, he rode back to the ranch house, went inside, found some jerky, some bread which was hard as a rock, and the empty water bucket.

He closed the door of the ranch house.

He went to the spring, filled the bucket with water, and rode back out to where the dog was still valiantly herding the sheep.

At a distance of about thirty feet from the dog, he dismounted and put the food and the water bucket down. He dipped the bread for a few seconds in the water to soften it, then he put it on the ground near the jerky.

*"Sorry dog,"* he said silently, *"it's all I could find."*

That dog, Mike thought to himself, fits my definition of a hero: *Do your best and keep going.* Valiant.

He mounted up and rode off, sure that the dog would not come to eat the food until Mike was out of sight.

Once over the slope, where the dog could not see him, Mike dismounted and crept back up to peek over the rise.

Sure enough, the dog had rushed over and was wolfing down the food in great gulps, not stopping to chew. The poor dog was starving. Then the dog began lapping up the water as fast as his tongue would go.

Mike watched for a few moments. The dog looked in his direction once, and Mike got the feeling that the dog knew exactly where Mike was, but had judged the situation was safe. The dog was between Mike and the flock.

Mike mounted and rode back toward the cabin. Once again, he rode past the closed door of the adobe ranch house and toward Aguardiente.

Maybe the sheep were the problem. Maybe someone wanted the sheep out of here so that cattle could be brought in. More and more since the war, longhorns were being herded and sold, moved north over trails like the one running up the Pecos. And a lot more valuable since the war.

Was that it? A longhorn was worth thirty to fifty dollars a piece up North, where they could be sold and shipped back East.

It had become big business since the war ended six years ago.

Cattlemen hated sheep. Said that they ruined the land for cattle. Even said that cattle didn't like the smell of sheep.

If it was that, though, why weren't the sheep killed, or at least run off?

And why was one man called a thief and run off and the other said to commit suicide with *three* bullets? Why not just murder the two men and have the bodies disappear, as Pierce had done with some other people who made him angry, according to Toothpick?

No. What had been done was done with some other purpose in mind. Done to *deliberately* attract attention.

But what was it?

The more he thought, the more he thought that it was not that Pierce wanted the Rushford place.

The place seemed abandoned. The spring was too small for a large herd of cattle.

What, then?

All of a sudden, Mike realized he was bone tired. He'd had no sleep last night, and this was a long day. It was hot. Real hot. He felt like finding a shady place and taking a nap.

There was no question of that.

Wade.

What had happened to Wade? He had secretly hoped that Wade would have ended at the Rushford place when he was backtracking. There was no evidence of this. No fresh horse tracks other than his own near the ranch house or the spring.

Mike hurried his horse forward. He was anxious to find out what Wade had discovered. Where Wade had gone.

But he had to find Wade first.

Where was Pierce now? Was he holed up somewhere close? If he could come and go that quickly to Aguardiente, he had to have a hideout nearby, didn't he?

## Chapter Seven

When he came into sight of Aguardiente, he realized again why Toothpick and Mocho were doing so well. Another wagon was parked outside of the adobe and a few new people were walking around the wagon and into Toothpick's place. More and more travelers and settlers were obviously passing though here, he saw as he rode toward Toothpick's adobe.

One lone man, with a horse beside him, was about ten feet outside of the livery stable door talking intently to Ted Buchanan, and Mike had the impression that the man was trying very hard to persuade Ted to hire him.

The man looked about nineteen or twenty, and had long, curly straw-colored hair. His brown hat hung from his chin strap down his back as he was talking to Ted.

Ted probably would hire the young man for next to nothing and let him sleep in one of the empty stalls in a blanket on a pile of hay.

As Mike rode his horse up to the hitching post, Ted was

nodding, somewhat reluctantly. Mike's best guess was that the young man was hired.

Cookie came out of the door of the 'dobe.

"Any sign of Jake or Wade yet?" Mike said.

"Nope," Cookie said. "Gettin' worried."

"Saddle up, and we'll take a look," Mike said.

Mike waited while Cookie entered the livery stable and came out a few minutes later. He was riding his old roan. Cookie liked his roan well enough, but the roan was not, well, a horse that Mike would want. He didn't have enough bottom—enough endurance—for here, where you might have to go a long spell without water.

Cookie probably knew that, but the roan was probably all he could afford right now.

At any rate, the old roan had done well enough today, so far, Mike thought. Perhaps he would be all right.

As Cookie rode toward Mike, Mike swung up onto his horse and together the two men set off, riding out of Aguardiente the way they had come.

As they rode, Mike told Cookie about the Rushford place, and about the dog.

"I think, like you said, Mike, that there's somethin' funny goin' on. Else Pierce would have just killed the Rushfords outright. Made them sign over the land, legal like, then shot them, buried the bodies out somewhere where they'd never been found. Tell everybody that the Rushfords sold them the land and that the Rushfords skedaddled back East with the money. Who'd ever been able to prove them wrong? What with the Rushfords dead an' all.

"I asked Toothpick when it was that Nat Pierce showed up first 'round here, and he says about a month and a half to two months ago,'' Cookie continued. ''He wasn't exactly sure.''

''Smart of you to ask. Should have asked that myself. Things've been happening kind of fast, Cookie,'' Mike said. There were a lot more questions he should have asked Toothpick, probably.

''You been busy, an' all,'' Cookie agreed. ''A lot's been goin' on kinda quick in the last few days. Hard to think straight.''

That was just like Cookie to say that. Cookie was always kind. Gave people the benefit of the doubt.

Mike and Cookie reached the spot where Wade had turned off. There were three sets of tracks heading off to the right. The original set, then Wade's, and then Jake's.

Then just over to the left, Mike and Cookie saw that there were two more sets of tracks that joined in from the left. Two more horses.

They looked at each other in surprise, then rode on, cautious but puzzled.

Mike was doing some heavy thinking: In an area that was so deserted that there was at least 130 miles of nothing but desolate, zigzagging trails between the *nearest* two army forts—between Fort Stanton and Fort Sumner—that so many people had been following this same trail . . .

The soldiers at both forts were there to deal mainly with Apache Indian troubles only. They wouldn't help with this. . . .

Cookie roused him from his wandering thoughts by saying, ''Shod ponies.''

He meant that he didn't think they were Indian tracks. Mike agreed.

They rode for another ten minutes until suddenly they heard gunshots in the distance. Mike and Cookie urged their horses forward.

Jake and Wade might need Mike and Cookie in a hurry. But as they rode forward, the shooting had already stopped.

Instead, Mike came upon a United States marshal—*what was he doing here?* And an Indian woman in a fringed deerskin dress—not an Apache woman—looked like more of a Plains Indian woman to Mike—pinned down behind a small rise. She was breathing hard, as if she had just run a good distance in a hurry. The lay of the land prevented them from getting away. After the rise, the land sloped down and then up again so that the two would have been in the direct line of fire had they left the small rise that they were pinned down behind.

Cookie looked at Mike for guidance: should go forward or not?

Mike waited, but the shooting seemed to have stopped, so he urged his horse forward slowly, his rifle out and ready.

Whatever it was, it seemed to be over.

The woman raised the rifle at Mike but put it down when he made no move to attack or hurt her.

After looking at Mike and Cookie and assessing them, she lowered the rifle further, and rested it across her knees where she was squatting, and silently pointed to the U.S. marshal.

The marshal, mortally wounded—gutshot—was next to the woman, about five feet away from the butt end of her rifle, to the left of the woman. The marshal's bulging saddlebags were next to him.

Mike had the feeling that the rifle belonged to the marshal.

The marshal was conscious. That was too bad.

The marshal motioned to Mike and Cookie to get down

off their horses. They dismounted instantly, and Mike said, "Cookie, you want to take a look-see?"

Cookie fell down on the ground next to the woman, and crept up the rise to peer over, keeping down as much as possible.

She moved the rifle away from his reach but copied what Cookie did, peering with him over the rise to see if there was any sign of whoever it was who had had the U.S. marshal pinned down.

They appeared to be gone.

"Looks like they vamoosed," Cookie said to Mike.

The marshal didn't have long. He knew it and Mike knew it, and so did Cookie and the Indian woman.

"Do me a favor," the marshal managed to say. "Get my paperwork on this back to Fort Stockton, Texas . . . money in saddlebag. Give it to her," he said.

Mike knew he meant the Indian woman. "She can hire someone reputable to take her home. See that she does. Followed me. Tried to get shut of her, but she wanted to get the man what soiled her, herself."

The marshal was in great pain, and his eyes were closed, but he held up a hand long enough to motion Mike to lean over close.

Mike did, and the marshal whispered, with great effort, "Don't . . . never call her squaw. She'll knife you in the gut if you do. Otherwise, she's a dang good woman. Lot of guts. Brave. In her language, *squaw* means a very bad, indecent word for down there," he motioned, clearly meaning private parts, looking up with great difficulty first to make sure that the woman was looking over the rise before he continued. "Terrible insult to call her squaw," the marshal managed to say. His eyes barely flickered open and he looked at Mike through narrow slits.

" 'Preciate it if y'd bury me, with my badge, before ya

moved on," he said weakly. "Everythin' else ya need to know is writ down. Writ even the last part, here, whilst we was pinned down. Writ it when I knew I was gut-shot.

"I was after a no-good ex-war profiteerer goes by the name of Nat Pierce." He pressed his hand flat onto his gut as if to hold it in. He blinked his eyes and then opened them once again with great effort.

"Sold government shoddy uniforms, cardboard shoes, spavined horses, bad weapons—durin' the war. *Got* to tell you . . . what I'm after him for . . . is Pierce escaped from prison in Texas. In there for murder. Killer."

He panted for breath, determined to continue. One hand was on the ground still holding on to his Colt, the other was pressed futilely over the bleeding wound.

"Him and his men bushwhacked me just now. Saw Nat Pierce clear—got a good look at him. Was him what shot me . . . in the gut.

Been trackin' him from Texas—with the Injun woman trailin' *me*—for over two months. Think he came here to . . ."

Here, the man's strength petered out finally, and he gave up talking, and living.

As he stopped breathing, the woman began an anguished, rhythmical chant.

Cookie looked over as if to say, *shall I stop her?*

*No,* Mike signaled Cookie, *let her be.*

Mike went through the marshal's pockets and removed everything he came across. He took the marshal's Colts— he wore a pair of them, and set them with the rest of the marshal's things, and he closed the man's eyes and folded his hands across his chest respectfully.

He motioned to the woman as best he could that she should take the money. Her face showed no expression, but her sharp eyes showed that she was watching very carefully what he did to the U.S. marshal, as she took the money.

She seemed to trust him in that she made no move to touch anything of the marshal's, her knife, or the rifle.

She kept on softly chanting; a song whose meaning only she knew. Mike suspected that the song was showing respect for the marshal.

Walking cautiously around the area in front of where the marshal had been pinned down, Cookie snuck out to see if there were any dead or wounded men out ahead of them.

When he returned he said he didn't find any signs of anything other than a place where there was evidence of men mounting up and riding away.

"Hard to tell how many," Cookie said. "They've vamoosed, anyways."

Mike and Cookie carried the marshal to a flat area and dug a grave and put the marshal in it; then they covered the grave with rocks. Mike did what the marshal had requested and buried him with his badge on.

Mike knew, by the tense, grave look on Cookie's face, that Cookie was aware that this was the *second* time that they'd done this same thing.

The woman, who had quieted down and watched as they piled rocks over the grave, began chanting again over the grave as the rock pile grew.

Cookie looked over at Mike, as if asking should he say a few words, too?

Mike shook his head.

This time, the woman was being the pastor.

Silently, Mike said a few prayers himself. He thought that perhaps Cookie was doing the same, as he had his head lowered, and his mouth was moving.

When the three of them were done, Cookie and the woman looked at Mike questioningly.

''Let's see if we can round up the marshal's and the woman's horses,'' Mike said.

He slung over his shoulder the saddlebag he had taken from the marshal and motioned to the woman to climb up onto Mike's horse.

Cookie got up onto his own horse.

Walking, Mike followed the trail of the horses. Sure enough, the marshal's horse had not gone far, and he located him in a few minutes of hunting. It was a large, good-looking black.

On a hunch, he whistled, and the horse came over. Another horse followed close behind the marshal's horse, as if afraid of being left behind.

The Indian woman swiftly got down off Mike's horse and, talking angrily in a language that Mike didn't understand, caught her own horse and climbed up onto it. She seemed to be scolding him—giving him a tongue-lashing—for getting the marshal's horse first.

It was another reminder that he was not good with women.

She was right. He probably should have gotten her her horse first. It was just that he'd spotted the marshal's horse first. It was nothing personal. But obviously, by her scolding, she didn't think that.

She'd had a hard day. Her ally, the marshal—even though he had seemed to be a reluctant ally—was dead.

Darkness had fallen but they rode back on their own trail for a few minutes, back away from the place that the shootout had been, before they stopped for the night, fifty yards off the trail, in the brush.

No one wanted to ride forward into an ambush in the dark.

Mike wanted to find Wade and Jake but the woman and Cookie would be at risk of walking into a trap if they didn't wait until morning before resuming their search.

Nat Pierce left a trail of death and destruction behind him. The burned man, the "suicide," and now a U.S. marshal.

It was not something necessary to discuss; no one had wanted to stay for the night at the place where they had buried the marshal. It was in a bad spot that the marshal and the woman had been caught; in effect, a trap. Pierce was no fool. Knew the area. Bushwhacked the marshal.

None of them seemed willing to risk a fire. No one mentioned it.

Cookie gave water to the woman from his canteen.

The moon came up.

As soon as it was feasible, without arousing the suspicion of the woman, Mike took Cookie aside and warned him about the "squaw" thing. He waited until she had gone off to relieve herself.

"You don't need to worry about *that,* then," Cookie said, vehemently. "I ain't about to call her no squaw!"

"You know where she's from?" Cookie asked, as he removed his saddle and that of the marshal's horse. "She sure ain't no 'Pache."

"No, but from up north, somewhere, by the looks of her clothes. Sioux, maybe."

"You think maybe Comanche?" Cookie asked.

"No. Not with that kind of dress." Mike said.

"You gonna take that rifle off her?" Cookie said. "Probably belongs to the marshal," he added.

"No," Mike said, chuckling. "*You* gonna take it from her?"

Cookie whispered, "Nope! Not me! Looks like she dang well knows how to use it, too!"

Cookie looked over at where she had disappeared into the brush and whispered again. "Never saw no woman before that's 'been soiled' that way. Feel kind of sorry for her. Kind of scared of her, too, to tell the truth. Looks fierce."

"She must be very angry, to follow Pierce as far as she has," Mike said.

"Wonder how far that was."

"No way of knowing. Doesn't seem to speak our language," Mike said. "But if Pierce was in jail in Texas, and the marshal was following him for two months . . . she may have been after him for years, for all we know. Pierce must have gone up to Sioux country after the war. Maybe we'll never know."

She came back out of the brush and sat down.

Cookie had heard all the marshal had said, all except the whispered information about the squaw business, so Mike didn't have to explain to Cookie what he was planning to do with the marshal's things.

"I'll take the first watch," Cookie said.

"Fine," Mike said.

It had been an incredibly long bad day. It reminded Mike of days during the war.

Mike laid his head on his saddle and drew his blanket around him, his gun beside him.

His eyes were just about closed, when he felt a very gentle push on his shoulder.

He opened his eyes quickly, alarmed, reaching for his gun.

It was the woman, pushing a round, cakelike object at him.

He took it, looking over in the pale moonlight and seeing that Cookie had been given one, too.

He put it in his mouth and took a bite, expecting a terrible taste, but instead it had a sweet, cakelike consistency.

He was barely through chewing it, and he was asleep.

## Chapter Eight

Mike spent a few precious minutes reading the U.S. marshal's day book as soon as it was light enough to read. It had been Mike's turn on watch, so he had waited until Cookie awoke before looking through the small book.

It was just as the marshal had told him. The marshal appeared to have no family. No wife and kids somewhere back in Texas. The book didn't say much else.

As he read, he looked up and noticed that Cookie was sharing his canteen with the Indian woman again.

In the pale yellow-gray early morning light, Mike poured a little water into his hat for Browny and then for the woman's grulla horse. Cookie did the same for his roan and for the marshal's big black horse. They would need to get the horses to water soon.

As soon as the light was good enough to track, the three of them saddled up.

The woman handed each of them another cake as they mounted.

They were off, riding first back to the trail, and then back toward the scene of the ambush. When they reached that area, Mike silently indicated that they would ride around it, and the others nodded.

As they circled around, Mike thought back over what the marshal had said about Pierce. He figured that the marshal's information was more reliable than Pierce's own version of what he had done during the war.

Spavined horses—horses with a bone disease which would cause the horse to go lame on you. Cardboard shoes. Sounded like a thing that a man like Nat Pierce might do.

His Uncle Marcus used to say ''In a hundred people, you find five or six who are bad. But boy, can they wreck things for the rest of us.''

His uncle was right.

He had never even seen Nat Pierce, but he was working up a terrible dislike for the man.

Not as bad as the dislike that the woman had, though, to make her do what she had done. It was incredible that she had come so far, was so persistent.

The marshal had seemed to think that it was time for her to give up, to be taken home.

Would she? Would she do that?

He looked over at her.

Cookie was being very nice to her, but she had no use, it seemed, for men.

It almost struck him funny, for a moment, even though it was not.

The irony.

She had no use for men, other than using them to help her get Nat Pierce, and he himself, just a few days ago, had sworn off women. Two of a kind.

But what Nat Pierce had done to her was a lot worse than what LuBeth had done to him. LuBeth had only hurt his pride.

Maybe his own troubles weren't as bad as he thought.

*I better stop talking to myself and watch the trail,* he thought, as they came to an area of rocks. *Bad habit, I have, of talkin' too much to myself.* In the rocky area, they had lost the trail.

The three of them spent a good while searching before they found the trail where the men had come out of the rocks.

It was Cookie that found it first. Just slight disturbances in the rocks, then a ways, and then a clear trail again as the rocks and pebbles gave way to dirt that showed tracks better.

It wasn't long after that that they came upon a canyon entrance.

The trail they had followed had been a long trail that didn't look like it connected anywhere to any of the main trails that Mike knew of in this region. This was a desolate area.

Cookie and the woman looked at Mike.

The trail was very faint here, but as far as Mike could tell, it didn't go into the canyon.

Still the woman sat on her horse and didn't move when Mike urged his horse forward, so he stopped, a few feet in front of her, and looked back at her.

The woman said something with no expression on her face to help Mike understand what she had said.

Finally he understood. Without moving her whole head— in fact with her head slightly down—she moved her eyes and raised her eyebrows slightly to indicate that Mike should do the same.

As he put his head slightly down, copying her, he looked out of the corner of his eye and he saw a very young Apache Indian boy to the right, up on a shelf on the canyon wall.

It would have been funny, if the sight of an Apache, even a small boy, did not strike terror in the heart. If there was a boy, then . . . how far behind was his father, uncles, and older brothers?

The young Indian boy was showing his bravery, and his utter contempt and disgust with the "white eyes," by sticking out his tongue at the three people forty or fifty feet away from him.

The boy had no gun or bow and arrow in his hands, only his pink tongue.

Was the boy the bait to tempt them to follow him into the canyon? Into a trap? Or was he a lone kid, trying to prove his bravery to himself by taunting two "white eyes."

Mike didn't want to pick a fight with any Apache, even a young boy. Especially a young boy.

What could he do?

Thinking quickly, he made a big show of taking off his new blue bandanna and putting a few small coins into it, then he tied it and threw it on the ground where the boy could see it. The blue showed up nicely against the dusty yellow earth here, making a good solid plop as it hit.

Then he waved to the boy, as Mike urged his horse on, past the opening to the canyon.

After looking at him oddly, the woman, and then Cookie, followed him.

Knowing that the woman didn't speak any English, and that Cookie wouldn't know what he was talking about anyway, he said to the woman, "I didn't have any penny candy on me."

Her eyebrows were still raised in surprise at his apparently bizarre behavior as she followed behind him.

The trail was hard to follow. Sandy dirt that filled in quickly over tracks here.

He had thought that, of course, the trail would circle around Aguardiente and end at the Rushford place.

He had, in the back of his mind, right from the beginning a picture that Bryce Rushford's son Jim had been home when the Pierce gang arrived the first time to kill his father.

That appeared to be a wrong assumption.

Wade and Jake would have arrived at the Rushford place by now if the son's tracks had led there, even going round about this way.

But had the burned man been instead taken to Nat Pierce's hideout? Had he known where their hideout was? Had he gone there to confront Nat Pierce about his father's death?

What about the man's boots by the bed, back at the Rushford ranch?

Had he been taken out of bed—bootless—and kidnapped and taken to the hideout? Probably. That seemed more likely.

Was it at the hideout that he had been stripped and the THIEF sign hung around his neck? Was that where Wade and Jake's trail, still backtracking Rushford's horse, was taking them?

And was Pierce and his gang *between* himself and Jake and Wade?

Yes. Jake and Wade had been further on by the time the marshal had been bushwhacked yesterday.

The woman spoke again. She stopped her horse.

This time she was pointing.

She was pointing at the ground. She seemed to be trying to tell him something. Something he himself had missed.

She got down, so did he.

Cookie stayed up on his roan, with his rifle drawn and at the ready.

She muttered and pointed and pretty soon Mike began to see what it was that she was telling him.

The tracks of many horses, surrounding two sets of tracks. They'd come up on Wade and Jake from behind, and surrounded them.

Dang!

She could read the tracks as clearly as if they were a story written on paper.

Jake and Wade had been captured here.

No sign of blood.

He tried to make her understand that the two men were his, by holding up two fingers and then pointing to and patting his chest over his heart.

She nodded.

She understood that the two men belonged to him, to his heart, she said, by holding up two fingers and then touching where her own heart was.

Then she walked around and studied the tracks and began holding up fingers, and touching her pointer finger at each of her fingers, and eventually she held up eight fingers.

Somehow, in the jumble of hoofprints, she had been able to tell that there were ten different horses, besides Jake's and Wade's.

*Jake! Wade!* He wanted to say, *Why did you backtrack the trail this far? When you saw that it was such a long distance from Aguardiente, why didn't you return for help?*

He knew why.

Loyalty.

Loyalty, as they reckoned it, to Mike himself.

He sighed, disgusted with himself, at how he had handled things.

He was furious with himself. He had bungled this thing badly!

"Cookie," he said, forcefully, trying to organize his

thoughts. ''Take this woman back to Aguardiente right now. Take the marshal's horse and all his things. Make sure that the woman gets back home, like the marshal wanted. Pay someone reputable to take her.

Make sure that the nearest U.S. marshal's office is notified of what happened and that the daybook gets back to Fort Stockton, Texas. The marshal's notes say that the daybook is to get to a man named Charlie Frick at Fort Stockton. I'm guessing that Frick is the marshal's superior.''

''No, I . . .'' Cookie said.

''Look, this is too important. You've got to do this. If you and I—and her—'' he looked at the woman—''get killed, there won't be anyone who knows the truth of what happened to that U.S. marshal. There *has* to be someone left alive who knows all that has happened. And that's you.'' He was not above using the woman, who he knew Cookie felt sorry for, to make his point.

''And if Pierce gets his hands on her—''

All of a sudden Cookie understood.

''All right, but after I do what you said, and take her back to Aguardiente, I'm coming back with help,'' he said. ''What are you going to do?''

''I'm gonna try some tactics I learned in the war,'' Mike said grimly.

He looked at the woman standing near him. If he raised his voice, he knew he would lose the ''silent'' argument. She was a woman who sat her horse high and proud, afraid of no man. And liking very few of them.

He pointed to himself and forward. Then he pointed to her and Cookie, and the marshal's horse and things.

He made motions to try to say that one man, him, with big guns, could sneak up on the bad men. He pointed to how much the dirt had been stirred up with three horses.

He tried to tell her Cookie was a good man. ''Very

brave,'' he said, pointing to Cookie. ''Take you to trading post,'' he said.

She shook her head.

He pointed to himself and then pointed to her and then said, ''Me get bad man. You wait at place where there's food and water.''

Then he made motions to say that he would come back to the trading post that had food and water and see her then.

He tried to make motions that indicated that she might make him get killed, trying to protect her. He was better off alone, he said, pointing to his own chest forcefully. He made motions to lay the guilt on her that she could get him killed by having to watch out for her.

She got back up on her horse.

Her face, until the end, had never shown any indication of any emotion, but before she left, she opened her saddle-bag and gave him three more cakes.

She said something as she handed them to him. It was probably something in the nature of ''Be careful,'' he guessed. Or maybe a curse word.

He took the cakes and said ''Thank you.''

She reached over and handed him the marshal's canteen, off the other horse, which he could tell had a bit of water left in it when he took it from her.

Finally, she reluctantly turned her horse and started back the way they had come. Cookie followed behind her, leading the marshal's horse.

''Cookie, make sure that dog at the sheep ranch gets some food and water,'' Mike called softly after him.

Mike had learned the marshal's name from looking at the daybook at dawn. His name was Alexander Granger.

## Chapter Nine

He was alone. Cookie and the woman were gone. It was a miracle that the Indian woman had agreed to go, although it had taken fifteen minutes of motioning and talking to persuade her. It hadn't been time wasted, but he regretted it all the same.

Jake and Wade were captured.

From here on in, he was on his own. Maybe it was just as well. Cookie was a kind, gentle person, and Mike wasn't at all sure that Cookie would be able to shoot a man. He was too young to have been in the war.

He was lucky that Jake and Wade had been taken alive. Either Wade or Jake must have done some mighty fancy talking. Probably Jake.

Cottonwoods. They told him that he had reached a river before he saw it. It was down in a gully about fifteen feet and the river water had a slight reddish tinge, but he dismounted, and climbed down and filled his canteen and his hat and brought them both back up.

The water in his hat he gave to his horse.

The horse drank two hatfuls before he was finished.

He drank some himself, and then he refilled his two canteens.

They had crossed the river here. Someone knew the river well. Knew that this was a good place to cross. He wondered if this was a river that, later on, emptied into the Pecos, to the east.

Without Cookie and the woman, he made better time, concentrating on the abundant tracks the large group made, but also alert, tense, his gun and rifle ready for ambush.

For being bushwhacked.

He was tense, his body on high alert.

Once, he looked back.

He thought someone had moved—in a bush—behind him. But he stopped, listened, and waited for at least five minutes, but he heard no further noise, so he rode on.

If it were Apaches, he'd already be dead with an arrow in his back, he thought.

Maybe it was a javelina, or a rabbit.

If it was a bushwhacker, he would be dead already.

A few minutes later, he reined in his horse and said, "I see you. Come on out."

He waited.

There was silence and no movement for a few minutes, and then the Apache kid came out of the shrubs, with the blue bandanna tied around his forehead as a sweatband, in the manner of Apaches in this area. He wore nothing but a breechclout, the bright blue headband, and high deerskin boots. The kid was lean and muscular, with a short, small, hawklike nose. A leather pouch hung from rawhide strings around his neck. Mike knew it contained his important religious objects and food.

Mike had seen the flash of the blue bandanna in the

shrubbery, but he didn't let on that that was how he knew the kid was there.

The kid seemed to speak good English. In fact, proper English.

He said, "How did you know it was me?"

"Just did," Mike said.

"Did I scare you? Were you scared?"

"Thought it was a rabbit, at first," Mike said grinning.

"A rabbit!" the kid said, insulted.

"Well, maybe a javelina," Mike said, smirking. "Once knew an Apache who I played a kind of "hide-and-seek" game with. I'd hide my eyes and give him five minutes with my back turned. Never could find him. Then he'd pop up right near my feet; he was buried in the dirt all the time right near me."

"He must have gotten *awfully* dirty and dusty," the kid said.

"Yep. Dirt and dust on everything—eyelashes, up his nose . . ."

"Ohhhh," the kid said disdainfully. "I don't think I'd like that."

"Why do you speak with a British accent?" Mike asked.

"My teacher, at the Fort, was from England."

Mike looked at the kid. He was very clean and neat. Even the new blue bandanna had been rolled and tied and folded and the ends tucked in very neatly.

Looked old enough to be thinking about girls.

Kid was in a tough spot. His culture told him he was supposed to steal things to show that he could provide for a woman.

If it were his own kid, he would say to the kid, "Just be a man who don't mind work." Here, there was nothing for the kid to work *at*. No jobs. Nothing to work at.

Kid was caught in a trap. If he stole, the white settlers

would get him. If he didn't, he was held as less than a man in the eyes of his friends and family. Mike didn't hold out much hope for the kid's future.

*No wonder Apache men sometimes became scouts,* Mike thought. *At least it was a job. Sometimes they became scouts against their traditional group's enemies, and sometimes, he'd even heard, to act as spies so that the Apaches being hunted would have information on the latest military strategies and plans.*

*Who knew, really?*

In any case, here he was with an Apache kid following him. It was the *last* thing he needed. And with a British accent, to boot.

"What do you want?"

The kid shook his head. "Nothing." The kid fingered the blue bandanna. "Where are you going?" the kid asked.

"After some bad men."

"After 'the people' . . . My people?" the kid asked.

"No. My people," Mike said. "White eyes."

"Oh, then I will help you track them."

"Too dangerous," Mike said. "Killers."

The kid faded back quickly, into the bushes.

"No!" Mike yelled. "Stay out of this."

"I am a brave warrior," the kid called in answer, already out of sight.

Gone.

"Dang!" Mike said loudly.

## Chapter Ten

For a day and a half, Mike had seen no other human being. He knew that the young Indian boy was out there. He had seen one small Apache moccasin print where he'd camped by a spring. He saw the print when he filled his canteen at dawn. The print had not been there last night. He knew that the kid was somewhere alongside him, out of sight. Nearby.

The boy was keeping up with Mike's horse, and he was on foot. That meant that the kid had not slept, but was making up for time by catching up while Mike was resting at night.

He'd heard of the amazing ability of Apaches to do this—cover so many miles a day—but he was just a kid . . . and, to tell the truth, Mike had done his best to try to lose him.

Mike had slept away from the spring in a carefully chosen place where he could not be seen, not because of the Apache boy, but because of Pierce's men. He'd kept out

95

of areas where he'd make a good profile for the same reason.

And last night, he'd listened, only half slept.

Browny had stood guard, in a sense, as he was almost as good as a goose as an early warning signal. He made noises if anyone came too close in the night, thinking that the lurker was a danger to himself. He'd nicker, or scuffle his hooves to wake Mike. His ears were better than Mike's for hearing things out there.

The night had seemed to pass too quickly. Mike was still bone tired, as he got up at dawn.

The trail he was following didn't seem to make any sense, unless it was just the trail of a group trying to lose someone; riding up and down streams, taking bends and turns, going across rocks, which left no trail, and going through sandy areas that fill in quickly when the wind is blowing, like it was now.

That is what had been going on for a day and a half.

Once, the Apache boy had left a trail marker—a message—of three rocks in a deliberate pile. One on top of the other, and a third rock in the direction that showed the kid had found the trail before Mike did. All out of sight of Mike, even though Mike knew the boy was close by.

If the kid was trying to impress Mike, he was doing it.

Mike wondered if the kid was doing it to earn money from Mike. Probably not. It was something else; more likely proving something to himself—that he was a good tracker.

He was.

Mike didn't know the boy's name. Probably Mescalero Apache, though, judging from the area he had been in when he ran across the Indian. You couldn't always tell, though.

Well, he'd pay the boy anyway. Cash on the barrelhead. When he saw him. *If* he saw him again. Would the boy fade away, once he'd tracked the whole trail to the outlaws Mike was seeking? Would he feel that he had proved his point—his manhood—by that?

Mike could only hope so.

They crossed back over the same river.

This told him something. Pierce had begun to close up a great big zigzagging circle.

Now Pierce was heading back, almost in a beeline, to the area near Aguardiente. He must have figured that he'd lost his pursuers.

A bullet winged by Mike's head as he rode up a slope. The bullet came from *behind* him. Bushwhackers had circled around behind to backshoot him!

Too late, Mike realized that Pierce had left outriders—guards—lookouts—behind.

He dropped down off his horse, rolling down to the ground and behind a large yellow limestone boulder.

How many were there?

At least two?

His question was answered as a shot came from the other direction.

Great!

One rock here, and two shooters. No matter which side of the large rock he went to, someone could sneak around to the other side and pick him off!

He got up onto his haunches, shooting in both directions, as he ran for the closest mesquite. At least out in the shrubbery he had a better chance.

As he ran, a bullet scraped across his shoulder. He looked, but there was only a rip in his brown shirt.

Then, he was behind the mesquite.

He thought that perhaps he'd heard an anguished shout as he knelt on one knee.

Had he hit someone?

He dang well hoped so.

He shot again and again using his Navy Colt, his rifle still in it's sheath on his gelding. Dang!

He quickly reloaded, filling all the chambers and shooting one bullet immediately just to show that he was not on empty.

Something Jake—good, dependable, steady Jake—usually said to younger cowboys popped into his mind.

Jake always said, "You gotta ask yerself *before* you get into a scrap. Did ya try everything else first?"

"Yes," Mike said with gritted teeth. "I did, Jake. But I gotta get you and Wade out of the fix I got you in!"

He needed to know where the Apache boy was before he shot at a bush directly in front of him that looked as if something behind it had just moved.

The darn smart Apache kid knew this and for a split second showed a bit of blue bandanna that only Mike could see. He had moved behind a bush to Mike's right. Dangblasted smart kid!

He shot then, at the bush directly in front of him.

Then he ran quickly to the right side, looking around and shooting as he went, trying to maneuver himself up a slope he saw in back of him, where he could get a better view of the men below him, hiding in the shrubbery on the flat.

He made it to the top of the slope and jumped over the top to safety, and looked down in back of him.

Surprisingly, there were two saddled horses in the gully behind him there.

He thought just a moment, then he got up and ran toward them, and taking off his hat, he swatted the closest one, a bay, on the rump with his hat, yelling "Go on, boy!" The other horse was a nice buckskin.

The startled horses took off, running rapidly, and soon were out of sight.

Good.

He ran quickly back up the crest of the slope to the top, dropped to the ground, and peered over from behind a shrub.

He whistled softly to his horse and Browny came up the slope toward him. As the horse reached the top and came over, Mike grabbed the reins and urged him up over the slope and down behind Mike to safety.

A shot rapidly slammed by him, but he knew that the shooters had heard their mounts running off and were aware, or at least guessed, that they would need Mike's brown gelding alive to get out of here.

He had gambled on that when he called the horse to him.

He shot a few more times into the mesquite where he thought the men were holed up; he had a lot of bullets left in his belt.

By now they should have scurried behind the rock where Mike had first been—it was the only rock around—and they hadn't—and that told Mike something.

They didn't appear to be too aggressively shooting at him, and he thought that that might mean that one of them was wounded and that the other one was losing some of his enthusiasm. He wasn't sure, but he thought he heard faint sounds that a quarrel was going on.

He had no love for these men, runnin' with Pierce.

A noise behind him almost scared the life out of him; and he whirled, knowing that if it was one of the two men—or even a third man—who had snuck around behind him, he would be dead in a few seconds.

His heart started to pound inside his chest.

He had to willfully stop himself, check himself, from pulling the dull gray metal trigger he held in his sweaty, tense-muscled hand!

It was the kid, leading the two horses that Mike had just shooed away.

The kid was grinning.

Not a bloodthirsty Indian, like so many people called those of his race, but a kid enjoying a good joke on Mike himself and the other two "bloodthirsty" white men.

He was saying to Mike without saying a word: "Let's take their horses and get out of here. Leave them on foot."

It was a chance for a delicious revenge on two back-shooters, the kid was saying by grinning like that and pointing to the two horses and Mike's own horse. No water for a long, long way. A day's ride to the nearest spring—or a day's steady run—if you were a young Apache boy, Mike thought to himself.

Seemed like a good idea to Mike.

He scrambled down the slope and swung up on his gelding as the kid swung up on the bay, leading the second horse, the buckskin, behind him.

They rode off.

Maybe the outlaws had heard the horse's hoofbeats, because one of the two outlaws ran to the top of the slope as he heard them ride off, yelling, "Git back here with them hosses!"

The angry man shot after them but it was no use, the kid and Mike and the three horses were around a bend made of sloping earth and out of sight in a few seconds.

The kid said nothing, never turned his head back to look at Mike, but Mike knew that the kid was probably pleased with himself and at how he had outwitted the stupid white men.

The kid had to know that there were a lot more "bad" white men in front of them, because he had been following the tracks, same as Mike.

Mike said nothing, either. He reloaded as he rode.

But he doubted that those partic'lar outlaws back there behind him would be bothering him again.

Would Pierce send someone back to see what happened to the two backshooters when they didn't return?

Now, it would pay to track slow and careful. Be on the watch for more backshooters circling around behind himself and the Apache boy. He slowed Browny down.

From the look of the boy's tense, straight back, he was as aware of this as Mike. But even if he knew, he gave no indication of being scared.

## Chapter Eleven

As they came to the top of each rise, either Mike or the boy took the time to get down and scout it out each time. They took turns, although neither had spoken aloud of it.

They were both still on the watch for riders circling back from Pierce's group.

But the group of tracks stayed the same. No sign that there had been any riders leaving the group.

As the hours passed, the two outlaws left back there were on their own, it looked like. Pierce wasn't sending anyone back for them.

The land was gradually rising, going upward.

Although the kid was generally riding behind him, once he rode deliberately in front of Mike and stopped, holding a hand up for silence.

Mike listened but heard nothing. The kid apparently did.

In a moment, the kid signaled for them to move on.

The kid was right. Evidently they were getting real close to Pierce and his gang. The tracks looked real fresh here.

Fresh horse dung in a pile here. They'd climbed up high in the last hour or so.

Mike loosened the rifle in it's boot. Checked and re-checked his handgun nervously.

The group had turned off into a downward winding trail. Into a canyon.

The hideout?

Yes. It looked as if they were heading to their hideout.

Layers and layers of ledges that water and wind were in the process of splitting apart were on each side of them as they rode slowly down the trail into the twisting and turning canyon.

Here, Mike didn't want to overtake Pierce.

He wanted to be able to scout around and plan before taking on this group of vicious killers. Wanted to make sure that Jake and Wade got out all right. He only hoped that Jake and Wade were all right . . . still alive when he reached them.

He didn't want to think of that; that Nat and Wade might be already dead. He didn't think so. Pierce would have simply left the bodies behind, wouldn't he?

Anyway, he needed to be careful.

He looked behind him where the kid was riding now.

The kid had no gun. No arrows. Only his wits and a knife. The kid had survived, so far, in a very hostile country.

As soon as it was rocky enough to cover their tracks, he and the kid rode off to the side of the faint trail into the canyon. It didn't appear to be a box canyon.

And as soon as Mike judged that they were coming to an area where the gang might be, he signaled to the kid to jump down and go behind a pile of rocks and hide and wait with the horses.

The kid did, taking the horses out of sight behind the rocks.

He was wrong. It *was* a box canyon.

Mike figured by looking up in the distance, toward where he could see the box canyon ended, that he was probably half a mile or so from where the gang was.

He guessed.

He wanted to be able to scout it out by himself, without worrying about the kid.

There were plenty of pinyon trees.

They must be high up.

There had to be a water source here in the canyon. He came to the edge of the trees, stayed hidden, and looked out.

He had come upon a clean, clear spring. It appeared, then flowed into a wash—a natural basin in the rocks, and then toward a group of cottonwoods and willows.

It was beautiful here. Good grass.

He did not dare to come out in the open. He would have liked to take a drink of the cool, clean, clear water. But a good distance away on the side of the spring was an unpainted house that had weathered to gray. Shacks and corrals were on the far side, back from the spring and the house. Saddles and saddle blankets were hung on the corral poles and some were on the ground.

Unsaddled horses were in the corrals, and a man was leaning on each corner of the house, each with a rifle.

The man closest to Mike was smoking, seemingly unconcerned, relaxed and at ease, even though he had been chosen to stand guard.

Evidently, they were sure that they were safe. Sure that the two bushwhackers had taken care of Mike. Didn't know about the Indian boy.

Good.

Mike intended to keep it that way.

He had to figure out a way to find and free Jake and Wade.

He made his way back to the boy.

He'd wait until nightfall, then get fresh water, and scout around some more. He wanted to keep the kid out of it.

Guarding horses was considered an important Apache job. He could probably get the young Apache to do that to keep him out of the ruckus when it came.

He needed to find out where Jake and Wade were being held. Could be in the house or any of the shacks.

In the meantime, he meant to ask the Apache boy his name.

## Chapter Twelve

"Hawk," the kid said. "That's what I am called."

Mike knew that he meant that that was what he was called on the reservation.

Apaches never told "White Eyes" their real Indian name. He wasn't sure, but he thought it was for a religious reason.

"That is a good name for you," Mike said. "You do have the eyes of a hawk," he said, truthfully.

Hawk looked pleased.

Hawk wanted to be the one who did the scouting around, but Mike managed to persuade him that he would be more useful making sure that the horses were not discovered, and killed, stolen, or driven away in the night.

Once, before dusk, the boy became alert and listened, and then relaxed again after a few minutes, a questioning look on his face, as if he were thinking, but he didn't say anything to Mike.

"What is it?" Mike asked.

"I think, nothing," Hawk said.

106

The moon rose by nine-thirty into a blue-black, clear, star-dotted sky. It was a three-quarter moon.

Probably just right for Mike's purposes.

Any fuller, and Mike's chances of being seen increased greatly. As it was, he needed to be very careful.

He needed, first, to get to the spring.

If he were Pierce, he'd have a man stationed near the spring.

It appeared Pierce was so confident that he didn't.

There was no sign of a guard as he slipped quietly to the spring, being careful not to let the two canteens clank together.

He filled the canteens, and brought them back to Hawk. Hawk borrowed Mike's hat to fill to use for the horses.

The last thing they needed was for the horses to start making noises that they smelled water nearby.

Mike left without his hat, leaving it for Hawk to use to water the horses.

He crept back toward the house. Still the two men—different men, judging from the shape their bulky shadows made—stood guard, but in the same places, at the corners of the house. They seemed to be paying no attention at all to the area near the spring.

That was fine with Mike.

He wanted to check the shacks first. Pierce was a man not likely to put prisoners in the best place—the house—he would keep that for his own comfort, Mike guessed—and hoped.

He had not reckoned with Jake's creativity and inventiveness.

As he circled the farthest shack from the house, he felt a presence next to him. He tensed up, ready to fight, expecting to feel a gun or a bullet in his back, but the calm, measured voice of Jake greeted him in a whisper instead.

''Yer ten minutes late, by my reckoning,'' Jake joked.

After Jake spoke, the two of them, by silent agreement, moved off a distance into the pinyon trees. When they were forty yards away from the shack, Jake spoke first.

''Figgered you to be here ten minutes ago. Man in there thought I was asleep. Gonna have a mighty big headache from the butt end of his own Colt come mornin','' Jake whispered. ''An' he's gonna miss this fine black-holstered, walnut-stocked Colt .44, an' ammunition belt, I'm wearing, too.''

''How did you know I'd be here?'' Mike whispered.

''On account of I know you so well,'' Jake answered.

''How did you get loose?'' Mike whispered.

''Trick I learnt in my misspent youth,'' Jake whispered back. ''When they tie you up, you swell yer muscles up big and tight, and you take a deep breath to make yerself bigger. Sometimes it gives you a little slack to work with . . . an' I worked with it.''

''You have no idea how glad I am to see you,'' Mike said.

Jake chuckled very softly in the darkness beside him.

Then he stopped. In the darkness caused by the trees Mike heard a change in Jake's voice.

''Wade,'' he said, worried. ''They cracked him over the head with a rifle butt, an' he ain't come to, yet, far's I know. They separated us. I was in the closest shed.'' Even in the darkness Mike could see he pointed to a shed. ''And Wade is over there to the left, in the place they use fer a combination blacksmith shop and saddlery. He was passed out when they trussed him up like a turkey and throwed him in there, shortly after we got here.''

Jake was silent for a moment, then he said, ''We got one break comin' to us, an' only one. Man in there,'' Mike knew he meant the shack he had come out of, ''is goin' to be out of it for a long while. An' he's tied up, and with my dirty ole bandanna stuck in his mouth, fer when he does wake up.

"The break I was referrin' to is that I heard Pierce's second in command, Ezra Porter, tell Shorty Sprague to stand guard in the shack that Wade is in.

"Now Shorty Sprague isn't such a bad guy, as varmints go. He tried to make them give Wade an' me some water, and to tell the truth, he's the one what tied me up so loose.

"I think that he's only with the gang because of some trouble he got in a while back when he got drunk. Seems like he's a good enough guy when he's sober—only gets mean when he gets drunk."

"Any liquor here?" Mike asked.

"Nope. Men were complainin' somethin' fierce 'bout that."

Their talking done, they edged back on out of the tree area slowly and carefully, Colts drawn and at the ready, and crossed, Jake leading, cautiously to the shed that Wade was in.

Mike slowly pushed open the door, and both he and Jake pushed quickly inside at the same time, guns drawn and ready to shoot.

A lone oil lamp lit up the small room, on a shelf above Wade's limp body.

Jake spoke first, as Mike knew he would, to the man, Shorty.

Shorty was extraordinarily tall, which didn't surprise Mike at all, given the usual man's idea of humor out here in the West.

Shorty had on black boots, black trousers, and a black-and-white checkered shirt. The nose on his unshaven face had been broken more than once, by the looks of it.

"Shorty, I think you might just want to light a shuck out

of here,'' Jake said, his gun all the time aiming at Shorty's heart. "Sure, Jake," Shorty said. "Mind if I keep my gun, so long's I keep my word?"

Jake nodded. Mike figured that Jake had sized up Shorty well enough so that Mike not only found himself keeping his silence, but also nodding his head at Jake's questioning look at him.

"Go," Mike said, waving his gun barrel toward the door of the shed.

Why not, if Shorty could be trusted to keep his word and get out of the canyon? One less man against them.

" 'Bout ready to leave this here group, anyway," Shorty said. "Thinkin' of takin' up the ministry, like my Pappy back in Tennessee."

In another second, Shorty was gone.

Shorty would be quietly saddling up his horse.

Mike hurried over to where Wade was lying on his side, on the dirt floor of the shack.

Blood was dried and caked on his right temple. There was a large swelling there. Wade didn't look good. He was very pale. Blood ran from the corner of his mouth; some dried, some more recent drips where he'd been punched.

Mike felt sorry and guilty that this had happened to Wade.

Between the two of them, Jake and Mike lifted Wade up and Mike put him over his shoulder. Jake stayed close by Mike's side, taking a second to blow out the lamp before they opened the door and left the shed, and then closing the door behind them.

Anyone entering the shed would think that the occupants were asleep for the night, and have to waste time lighting the lamp to find out any different. As the shed was quiet, there might be no reason to check it the rest of the night.

They made their way back to where Hawk and the horses were.

## Chapter Thirteen

If Jake was surprised to see an Apache Indian boy taking care of three horses in the pale moonlight, he gave no sign of it.

Mike put Wade gently on the ground. He could be dying, for all Mike could tell. He showed no signs of waking up or stirring. Once again, Mike dribbled water from his own canteen into an unconscious man's mouth, almost sick to his stomach that it was Wade. He swore.

Brutality followed Nat Pierce.

Mike was so angry at Nat Pierce and his gang that he wanted to go and get him right now. He stood up.

"Jake, I'm goin' back to the house back there after Pierce now," he said.

In the moonlight available, Mike couldn't see Jake's face, but he could hear the surprise in his voice. Jake was standing next to him as he said, "But he ain't here, Mike. He just came to the hideout to drop us—Wade and me, and the four guards—off. He left a couple of hours after he got here. Went back to the Aguardiente area."

So that was what Hawk had heard. Men riding out, in the distance. Probably hadn't mentioned it because he didn't trust his gut feelings. *Always trust your gut feelings,* Mike said to himself. He should have questioned the kid more. It was probably his own fault for not questioning Hawk.

Well, that answered one question that had been nagging at him; why it had been so easy to rescue Wade, and get Jake away. And why there was no guard at the water. And why the guards had been so relaxed.

The boss was gone.

*What should I do now?* Mike asked himself.

As he was thinking, he noticed that Hawk gathered up all the canteens, with a silent glance at Mike for permission, and disappeared. In a few minutes he was back, and he put a filled canteen back on each horse.

Mike was thinking.

If Pierce was gone, did he need to stay here and fight the two men—the other two guards—who were left?

Or was his responsibility to Wade, Jake, and the kid?

Wade, clearly. First and most of all, right now.

He made his decision.

They could go back and steal a horse, but there was no way that Wade could ride alone, anyway.

They had the buckskin for Jake to ride.

"Help me get Wade up on my horse," Mike said, and once again, Mike was riding with an injured man being held onto the saddle by himself. *This is getting to be a habit,* he thought bitterly.

Hawk went first, trusting his own eyesight for traveling at night better than either Jake or Mike did.

Hawk led the way back out of the twisting canyon.

Once Jake rode close to Mike and asked, "Thought that 'Paches didn't travel at night. Spirits of the dead supposed to be out an' all that. And supposed to be afraid of rattlers that hunt at night.''

''Don't believe everything you hear,'' Mike said.

He smiled in the dark as he thought about the first time Jake would hear the Apache boy's British accent.

Once out of the canyon, they were in no rush. The moonlight was working in their favor here.

It was probably only an hour or two back to Aguardiente, and there was no need to get there tonight. In fact, as soon as they were safely out of the canyon and away from the two guards left, they needed to stop as soon as possible; all the bouncing and jiggling on the horse wasn't doing Wade any good in his condition.

''Over to the right, there's a good *trinchera,*'' Jake said, a few minutes later, obviously thinking the same thing as Mike.

He meant a position that could easily be defended, a fortified position.

They rode over to a place where steep rocks were at their back and there was a circular slope leading to a place they could easily defend, as well as hide the horses from sight. There was even the outline in the dark of a scraggly tree there. It still might provide some shade if they were still there after daylight.

Getting down from their horses quickly, Hawk and Jake helped get Mike get Wade down.

''I'll take the first watch,'' Jake said. Although they were probably safe for the night, no one moved to unsaddle the horses.

Hawk must have been exhausted, but he moved off a bit from Jake and himself and Wade and disappeared, probably to sleep.

Mike dribbled a bit more water between Wade's lips before he lay down to sleep.

In two hours, Jake woke Mike. Mike and Jake alternated turns on two-hour watches the whole night.

Wade's condition hadn't changed by first light.

At dawn, Jake used his hat again to water the horses.

Just after dawn, Mike was up on his horse again with Wade in front of him. Jake was riding the outlaw's buckskin.

And Hawk was gone. So was the bay Hawk had been riding.

Hawk had no intention of going to Aguardiente.

Mike didn't blame him.

He wondered if that was the last he would see of Hawk. And he wondered if Hawk had a family.

Hawk had been a big help, Mike thought.

Perhaps the big bay would help him in his quest for a woman.

He hadn't had a chance to pay him.

*Good Luck, Hawk,* Mike said silently.

Mike did some more thinking as they rode quietly without further incident into Aguardiente, holding Wade gently and carefully in front of him as he rode. It had been a four-hour ride into Aguardiente. Longer than Mike had thought.

Wade's head hung down and bobbed up and down gently in front of him as they rode. Luckily they were heading so that the sun shone on the top of Wade's hat as they rode.

He knew Jake was feeling just as bad as Mike did about what had happened to Wade.

*And it's all my fault,* he thought to himself.

What had happened to all his plans for being footloose?

He hoped that Toothpick had sent for the sheriff, as he said he would.

Mike had a new idea about why Pierce had done what he'd done to the Rushfords.

## Chapter Fourteen

They must have been watching for his return, because Mocho and Toothpick hurried out of the door immediately and rushed to help carry Wade into the back room—their own private living area—of the adobe, behind the curtained doorway in back of the counter.

Mike and Jake waited in the front room anxiously.

Mocho came out shortly, shaking her head sadly, no.

"Is he dead?" Jake asked, worried.

"No, but he's bad off," Mocho said. "An' he's a nice guy, I think." With that, she returned to the back room.

When Toothpick came out a few minutes later, he gave a thumbs-down sign to Jake and Mike. He looked worried.

He came over and sat down. They followed him and sat down to talk.

"I think he's in what they call a coma," Toothpick said. "Jest have to wait an' see. Cookie came back here with Red Hands and tole us about the U.S. marshal an' all. Looks like you fellers been busy."

115

He smiled slightly, more with his mouth than with his eyes.

"Cookie's been busy, too. Seems he and the lady Injun are gettin' sweet on each other. Seems he's thinkin' of askin' you if you'd mind if he took her north himself. They been makin' camp out behind the store."

*Red Hands? Was that her name?*

Mike looked at Toothpick.

"I'd be glad if someone got some happiness out of this mess. An' it's his decision, anyways. I'm not his boss anymore."

He thought, *With what I've done to Wade, I don't deserve to be anyone's boss anymore.*

Toothpick sat up straighter in his chair, as if to say that what he was going to say next was more serious business. He leaned forward and talked more softly, as if he didn't want Mocho or anyone else to overhear.

"Sent fer the sheriff like we planned. But I think I got it figgered out. Think that Pierce did what he did to the Rushfords on purpose. Think he did it *to get the sheriff over here.* An' it's working. He's coming. He was away on business—a day's ride from home, but the man I sent over to Calabasa to get him said they got the message to him all right.

An' if I know U.S. marshals, as soon as they get my message—and git the marshal's daybook—they'll send someone, too. I sent it on to Fort Stockton like you said to.

"Sent the new feller that was workin' at the livery stable. Seemed glad to go. Didn't like shovelin' out stalls none. Didn't like horses much neither. Let him take one of my wagons; gave him money and supplies fer the trip. Poor Ted Buchanan—had to hire a *new* jasper that come into

Aguardiente two days ago. Wish we had a telegraph 'round here, or at least closer.

"The feller that left is goin' to telegraph the U.S. marshals' office the first place he comes to that has a telegraph—'course, gettin' the daybook to them will take a mite longer—he's gonna bring them that. I tole him don't turn that over to *nobody* but Charlie Frick in Fort Stockton. Jasper is trustworthy—I hope. Should have reached there by now."

Toothpick paused to roll the toothpick around in his mouth, thinking. Then he said, "I bet they—Pierce an' his gang—aren't countin' on what you did, letting us git the marshal's daybook back to Texas.

"They must figger that they're plumb safe now, thinking that that marshal died out there alone, way the heck out here in New Mexico Territory and not even back in Texas where he come from.

"Probably gettin' awful cocky, 'cause they already got away with so much around here."

Toothpick seemed to be saying that he thought Pierce's group had no knowledge of the Sioux Indian woman being with the marshal during or after the gun battle.

Toothpick must have been able to talk, or communicate, somehow, with the Sioux woman. And somehow he had learned her name.

Toothpick shrugged, reluctantly.

And he was right. The Sioux woman was probably not known to the Pierce gang, or they would have killed her, too.

Mike had already had the feeling that the woman had been out of sight when Pierce's gang struck the marshal. Now, Toothpick seemed to be supporting that theory by what he had just said.

She *had* been breathing hard, as if she had just been

running, when Mike first saw her. So maybe she had been out of sight of Pierce's men. Maybe they were not aware of her existence, as Toothpick seemed to think. If they had, certainly they would have never left her alive . . . and undamaged . . . and with what had happened to her before when she came in contact with Nathaniel Pierce, she had shown a lot of courage . . . and maybe a lot of faith in that marshal she was following . . .

Toothpick interrupted Mike's thinking when he said, ''The next U.S. marshal will be some time gettin' here, anyways. But the important thing is that I sent fer the sheriff. He's on his way . . . It's the sheriff that Pierce wants. But maybe this time, Pierce bit off more than he can chew.''

New Mexico Territory—and Aguardiente—was a fairly long way from Fort Stockton, Texas . . . but when one of their own was killed, Mike doubted that distance would make a bit of difference to them.

They'd come after the dead marshal's killers right away. Top priority. And Pierce *was* an escapee from a Texas jail.

''Funny you should say that,'' Mike said. I was thinking the very same thing as I rode back here. I was thinking that Pierce has some grudge against Sheriff Rushford.''

''Where do you think Pierce is now?'' Toothpick asked.

''I'd say that he's waiting somewhere on the trail from here to Calabasa, waiting to bushwhack Sheriff Rushford. Knows or probably guessing which trail Rushford'll take.''

''Well,'' Toothpick said, ''if the sheriff has had some previous bad blood with Pierce, it stands to reason that the sheriff'll figger that out hisself.

''An' Sheriff Rushford, if he gits here all in one piece, has another surprise waitin' for him. Someone arrived whilst you was gone. His niece. Bryce Rushford's daughter by a previous wife. Gossip has been that he had two wives, one here and one back in the States.

"Knowin' Rushford, I don't think that that is true.

"Young woman who says she's Bryce Rushford's daughter arrived a little while ago. Over at the stable now, gettin' ready to ride out to the sheep ranch. It's hers now, I guess.

"All upset when Cookie tole her about the dog out there alone. Bought some vittles fer the dog here at the store. Gonna take them out with her to the ranch.

"Trouble is, she's in such a hurry and I ain't had no chance to talk to her at all. Headstrong. Close-mouthed little thing she is, too."

"It might not be safe for her out there right now." Jake said, worried.

"That's what I was thinking," Mike said, standing up.

"Mocho tole her that rather strongly. Tole Mocho to mind her own business. She's one stubborn headstrong lady. She's in the livery stable right now," Toothpick said. "Went over there not five minutes before you arrived in town."

"You goin' to see fer yerself?" Toothpick asked as Mike walked to the door.

Mike glanced once at the curtain to the back room. He didn't want to leave Wade.

"Don't worry none about Wade," Toothpick said. "Mocho's 'bout as good a doc as we got in these parts. She's takin' good care of him. Washin' him off now, as we speak. If you can catch the fiery little filly, tell her that she can stay here with me an' Mocho until things get settled down at her ranch."

Jake looked at Mike. "Go do what you have to do. I'll help with Wade if they need me. And when you're through, please look up Cookie out back and see if you can talk some sense into him.''

As Mike went out the door, he realized that Jake was upset. He didn't blame him. Things had turned into a mess since they had left LuBeth's.

Wade was hurt, maybe dying. And obviously Jake thought that Cookie was making a big mistake. Or Jake just didn't want a woman to break up their little group of friends heading to El Paso together. And Pierce needed to be dealt with. And this woman . . .

## Chapter Fifteen

W hen Mike saw what was happening, he didn't have time for niceties. He said quickly, "Get down off that horse."

The lady, riding sidesaddle because she wore a dress, was sitting on the horse in front of the livery stable. Her dress hung down on the opposite side from Mike and he could clearly see the belly and chest of the horse.

The woman looked surprised and more than slightly alarmed.

She had a large burlap bag of supplies hanging next to her, and her saddlebags were obviously full.

"Get down off that horse," Mike repeated.

She swung down off the horse, but she looked frightened and almost ready to cry.

"Are you a horse thief?" she asked, scared, but still standing with her back straight and defiant.

Mike walked over and unbuckled the cinch, poked the horse in the barrel of his stomach with his arm. The horse's stomach reverted to a normal size. The air the horse had been holding inside as he was holding his breath whooshed out.

"Cinch was too loose," Mike commented, as he rebuckled it correctly. "Before fifteen minutes went by, you'd have been riding, hanging upside down clinging to that horse's belly like a sleeping bat, and your head would have been bumping along the ground. Who saddled that horse?"

The woman looked greatly relieved that her horse was not being stolen out from under her.

"I don't want to get the man in trouble," the woman said, reluctantly. "That's why I don't want to say which man saddled my horse."

"Oh, that explains it," Mike said, sarcastically. "Sorry, but I got to go and have a talk with that man before he goes and gets somebody killed. Wait here a minute."

Mike left, walking toward the livery stable door.

"I have a feeling," the woman said to the horse, and looking at Mike's angry, retreating back as she remounted, "that the man who first saddled you up is in for a surprise."

Inside, Mike was already dressing the new stableman down when Ted came over. He knew it wouldn't have been Ted. Not mincing any words, Mike told Ted what happened.

"You could've got Miss Rushford hurt," Ted said sternly to the man. "What the hell's the matter with you this morning?" Ted said. The man looked like he drank too much, as a general rule. Mike could smell liquor on his breath.

And as Ted made a face when he came close to talk to the man, he knew Ted had smelled it, too.

Ted said to Mike, "Sorry. He never did anything like that yesterday. He's only been working here two days."

Mike had a feeling that this day would be the man's last

day working at the livery stable, as he heard Ted begin to dress the man down further as Mike walked toward the stable door. He clearly heard the word *out* as in ''Get out!''

Walking back out the stable door, he came to where the lady sat, back up on the horse.

He took a closer look at her. She wore a cotton sunbonnet which had tiny blue flowers all over it that matched her dress—and her eyes—exactly, and her shiny black curls peeped out from underneath the bonnet all around except for the area where her face peeked out. There was a large, perky bow of the same material under her chin.

She had short, capable-looking fingers that held the reins awkwardly, as if she wasn't used to riding that much, but her hands looked as if they'd done their share of work.

''Usually ride in a wagon?'' he asked.

''Yes. Usually,'' she said. ''My name is Annie Rose Rushford,'' she said formally, holding out her hand.

He took it and shook it politely.

''I was raised by my aunt in Kansas.''

He grinned. ''Mike Conroy. I was raised by my uncle in Texas,'' he said. ''Looks like we might have something in common.''

''Mike Conroy! Cookie told me all about you yesterday,'' Annie Rose Rushford said. ''Said all the women like you right off.''

''Not true,'' he said firmly, thinking bitterly of LuBeth Atkinson, and then about the Indian woman scolding him.

''Cookie said that your last girlfriend was no good,'' Annie Rose added. ''That's too bad.''

''Cookie told you all that?'' Mike asked, mildly annoyed. That was unlike Cookie.

''How did you even know about me at all?'' Mike added.

''Well, I heard everybody saying Mike did this, and

Mike did that, and Mike said this and Mike said that, and I got curious, so I figured that I'd ask Cookie about you. So I did.''

She turned, and took up the reins, ready to leave. Then she turned back.

''I heard what you did for Bryce—my father, that is—and for my half-brother Jim. And for the dog. Thank you. Thank you very much for all that you've done. And thank you for the cinch business . . . and just to set things straight, the rumor that you've probably been told about my father having two wives at the same time just isn't true. My mother died when I was born. She was his first wife. That's why I was raised by my aunt. I'm—I was—only two years older than Jim. My father married again rather quickly, you see.''

''Please don't worry about it, Miss Rushford,'' Mike said. ''I'm sorry about your troubles.''

Why was his heart pounding like this? He wasn't frightened.

She was sure a quality lady; not like a certain other woman he'd known. What a pretty name. Sweet Annie Rose. Sounded like a song. Sweet Annie Rose.

Looked awfully smart, though. And talked like a schoolteacher.

Said ''and'' with a ''d'' on the end and ''told'' instead of ''tole.''

Didn't seem snooty, though. Just grateful. And factual.

He wondered if he should send Jake out to watch over her.

Toothpick said she could watch out for herself, but he wondered. Especially when she didn't even know about cinches an' all.

*And* all, he corrected himself.

"Wait," he said, hurrying after her. She was heading slowly toward the trail north.

She seemed glad to stop.

"How much you know about horses?" he said.

"Not too much," she admitted. "Treat them firm and fair and feed them well," she said, as if she was reciting from a school book. "No sudden movements. No rough treatment."

She seemed finished, then she added what seemed to be from a book she'd read on the subject: "What you got to watch out for is frightening a horse. When a horse is scared he's no great thinker. He gets addle-brained," she said, "kind of like some people," she added. "I like horses, Mr. Conroy, even though I'm no expert. Horses can be gentle and friendly, like some *people,* once you show them *they don't have to be scared.*"

Mike had a feeling that she was talking about more than horses.

Was she talking about him? Was she saying for him not to be afraid of her?

Why should he be scared of her?

She was just a little bit of a thing, in her blue-flowered dress and pretty pink cheeks.

Well, all right. Maybe he was scared of her. Just a little. Scared that she wouldn't like him. Or laugh at him.

Or think him a darned fool.

Which he sometimes was. Recently, a lot.

"I can't go out with you," he said, meaning to the Rushford's sheep ranch.

She looked shocked and insulted. She raised her delicate eyebrows. Her mouth dropped open a bit in surprise.

"I never asked you to," she said.

"No, I meant to your ranch." he said, his stomach dropping as he realized that he was handling this poorly, as usual.

"What I meant was, that it isn't safe for you to go out there alone *right now*." he said.

"Oh," she said. She thought a minute. "But *you* did. Cookie said you went out there."

"You might be walkin' into a shoot-out," he said. "Your uncle is on the way here. He might go to the ranch first. We think he's the reason that your father was killed and your brother was . . ."

"Was brutally burned to death by the July sun here?" she said, not mincing words, in fact trying to shock him to show how unafraid she was.

Good act, good bluff, but he had seen her hands trembling when he had told her to get down from the horse.

"Please, Miss Rushford. Your journey can wait a bit longer. Cookie's been taking care of your dog. We need to talk a bit, first."

That was only partly the truth; his real reason was that he didn't want to leave Wade right now.

Reluctantly, she dismounted. He took the reins and led the horse to the hitching post in front of Toothpicks's store and tied him there.

Surprising him a little, she quietly followed.

But what surprised him the most was the expression she had had on her face when her uncle had been mentioned. She had tried to quickly cover it up; but it was clear—he'd seen it anyway—that she did not like her uncle.

Why?

And why was she not surprised to hear that it might have been something her uncle had done that had caused the tragedy that happened to her family?

They walked inside and sat down at the third table, near

the back, where the two women, Mabel and Alice, had sat with Rusty.

Mocho, Toothpick, and Jake were in the back room, he guessed, as there was no sign of them.

"Well?" she said.

"How much do you know about your brother, and your father, and your uncle, the sheriff? And especially, what do you know about Nat Pierce?"

"I know what happened to my brother and my father, and what you and your group did about it, and I know that the sheriff—my Uncle Clarence—killed Nat Pierce's brother Jeff over a year ago, in Texas somewhere. Pierce has a big family; lots of brothers and cousins on both sides of the family.

"My uncle wasn't even acting as a sheriff. He was just visiting some of our relatives—another brother—and he was a passenger on a stagecoach being robbed.

"Jeff Pierce was killed during that holdup, I think. Trying to rob a coach that that my uncle—the sheriff—just happened to be riding on.

"Nat Pierce was in jail in Texas at the time, but he swore that he'd get my Uncle Clarence—kill him—for killing Jeff. Anyway, nobody worried much about it, because Nat was in jail then. Was in for life, I think, for murder. And my Uncle Clarence can take care of himself. Always has. Don't think too many people outside of both families even knew about the incident."

"Have you ever been here before?" Mike asked, not needing to know this but just curious about the woman.

"Yes, a few times, while I was growing up. Just to visit. My father thought it was too rough out here for a young girl. Too many men and not enough women around.

"And scared of what the Apaches would do, if they got ahold of me. Too dangerous, he thought." Her expression

gave Mike the feeling that she hadn't agreed with her father's assessment of the situation and that she would rather
have lived here with him and her half-brother than back in
Kansas.

"Toothpick tell you that Pierce showed up here a while
ago?" Mike asked.

"Yes. He said he showed up here a few months ago.
Said he was very dangerous. A 'bad hombre,' I think he
called him."

"Do you realize that Pierce could kidnap you and use
you for bait to get your uncle? Especially if you go out
alone to the ranch."

"No. I never thought of that," she said alarmed and a
little angry. "A gentleman . . ."

"Nat Pierce is no gentleman! Don't make the mistake
of thinking that!" Mike said. In his mind he pictured only
too clearly what the sunburned man on the horse looked
like, and about the father shot in the back . . . and the Sioux
Indian woman.

He could see that he had put some new thoughts into her
head, even though she appeared angry. He guessed he had
kind of yelled. He guessed she wasn't used to being talked
to like that.

It was true, most Western men wouldn't think of harming
a lady. But Pierce was not a man who lived by the rules
of decency. And it was different out here. It was wilder, a
harsher land than she was used to.

Lord only knows what she'd do if she had to deal with
Apaches.

"Sorry, I didn't mean to yell," he said.

Reluctantly, she said, "Then you believe that for the
time being, I should stay here with Toothpick and
Mocho?"

He nodded.

"Just until we get this business with these outlaws straightened out. Even now, Toothpick says that your uncle is on his way here. Cookie's been out to see about the dog."

He hadn't asked who it was that Toothpick sent to Calabasa to fetch Sheriff Rushford. Probably some local man—some unlucky rancher who had come into Aguardiente for supplies. He had sent the first livery stable helper to notify the U.S. marshal's office; the one Mike had overheard getting hired.

Yep, probably some unlucky rancher who had come into the store to get supplies.

Mocho came out of the back room and walked over to Mike.

"Think Wade's a little better, Mike," she said.

Mike sighed with relief.

"Not awake yet, but color better and breathing better and eyes—eyes go like this," Mocho said, demonstrating using her own eyes to show fluttering motions.

"He's beginning to blink?" Mike asked.

Mocho smiled and nodded yes.

"Thanks, Mocho."

She smiled and went back into the back room.

Mike was greatly relieved.

"I need to go and talk to someone," Mike said. "Will you be all right if I leave you here?"

"Certainly."

He left Annie Rose sitting there while he went outside to find Cookie and see what was going on with him.

Outside, he walked north along the front of the building to the edge of the plank porch and around toward the back of the adobe.

## Chapter Sixteen

As he came around the side of the adobe, he saw the dwelling that Cookie and Red Hands had designed. It was forty feet back and to the left of the adobe, behind some chicken coops.

It was kind of comical. Together, Red Hands and Cookie had built something halfway between a wickiup—which was the kind of Apache Indian dwelling that Cookie knew about and had seen—and the teepee design that Red Hands was familiar with from the north.

It was a partially skin-covered brush dwelling in the domed-shape of a wickiup. It had a hole in the middle of the top and the skins had some designs painted on them that Mike had never seen. He assumed that they were Sioux designs.

The door had a flap pulled back, made of skin, so that privacy could be had when necessary. Mike had seen Sioux teepees and he guessed that Red Hands had contributed that part of the design of the structure.

He would have liked to see the inside but it appeared that the Indian woman was not at home.

Cookie saw Mike and hurried over, embarrassment clearly showing in his demeanor. Mike met him halfway.

He obviously felt awkward at seeing Mike.

''Anxious to talk to you,'' Cookie said, turning as he reached Mike and walking back with him toward the brush dome. He was nervous, Mike thought, about telling Mike that he wasn't going with him to El Paso.

Mike wanted to reassure Cookie as soon as possible.

''Good to see you,'' Mike said. ''How's everything going?''

Cookie hesitated and then said, ''Well enough I suppose.'' He looked toward the brush structure and then at Mike.

''Want you to know that I am sleeping out yonder. This aint' fer me *and* Red Hands. Just fer her. Just want you to know everything is on the up and up betwixt me an' her.''

Cookie was worried about Red Hand's reputation.

''Never thought otherwise,'' Mike said. ''Never knew you to be anything other than a gentleman.'' That was the truth.

Might as well get it over with and put Cookie's fears to rest.

''I hear that you're thinkin' of escorting Red Hands back up north to Sioux country,'' Mike said, in a relaxed manner.

Cookie looked very relieved that he didn't have to do the telling.

''Thinkin' on it,'' he admitted. ''Haven't mentioned it to her yet, though.''

''Red Hands showed a lot of courage,'' Mike said, ''doing what she did.'' He meant trailing Pierce and the marshal; not to mention trailing Pierce all the way down from Sioux territory in the first place. That was an incredible feat.

Cookie nodded.

"By the way, about her name," Mike said. "Isn't that an unusual name?"

Cookie looked embarrassed again. It was clear that he didn't particularly want to tell this to Mike, but felt that he owed it to Mike to be honest. "It's . . . that's not her real name. Her real . . . Sioux name is "Woman Who Cries At Night," on account of what happened to her. She has renamed herself Red Hands. She says that that is what she's going to call herself until she can kill Pierce with her own hands—the Red part of her name stands for the blood that she'll have on her hands the day she gets her hands on him. It's kind of a—like a reminder to her of her blood vow."

Cookie looked sorry and sad as he said this. He looked off in the distance as he spoke, as if he didn't want to look Mike in the eye as he talked.

"The thought of that kind of makes me sick to my stomach," Cookie said.

Mike was both surprised and not so surprised. He'd thought—hoped—that she was willing to go home with Cookie right away, but the thought of what Red Hands might mean *had* crossed his mind.

"You ought to try and get her to go home. Tell her that I will make it my *duty* to take care of Pierce. Tell her it's time for her to let someone else take over. She's done her part. She's done enough."

Cookie, nodded, relieved.

"I'll tell her. Hope she'll listen." Cookie's voice expressed doubt that she would.

As they talked, Mike and Cookie had wandered back to

the edge of the plank porch in front of the adobe. They sat down on the corner.

"That reminds me. How do you talk—communicate with her?"

"She talks. She speaks what she calls 'white people talk.' She says you never asked her, so she never said. Kind of enjoyed watchin' you struggle, she said, pointin' out yer heart and all; that time. Struck her mighty funny. Said she could hardly not laugh right out loud, except things were so serious at the time. Began talkin' English to me right after we rode off. I thought of ridin' back an' tellin' you, but you were sure busy enough, an' I thought it more important to keep on going back to Aguardiente and tell about the marshal an' the daybook an' all.''

Mike stood up and he and Cookie wandered back toward the wickiup.

Mike was curious. He wanted to go inside the unusual dwelling and look around, but there was still no sign of Red Hands, and he would never go inside unless he was invited.

Cookie suddenly realized that Mike was looking around for her and he said, "She's gone out looking for food. She finds things to eat out there." He pointed to the desertlike area surrounding Aguardiente. "Indian things. She has survived for a long time on her own."

Mike nodded. She probably used snares.

She had survived the arid conditions out there that went on for miles and miles—seeming like forever—and the areas with nothing but cactus, clumps of grama grass, and mesquite. And little water. And before that she'd come down from the Great Plains by herself into Texas, and then here.

All by herself.

Trailing that scoundrel.

Cookie added, ''I don't call her Red Hands. Don't rightly say as I care for that name. She's got a right to call herself whatever she wants, of course, but I call her Woman Who Cries At Night, an' she's all right with that.''

''Make sure you tell her what I said,'' Mike said.

''I'll tell her and I'll be sure an' tell her that she can trust you; you're a man of your word. Although I think she's figgered that out for herself already.''

''Thanks, Cookie.''

''I don't think that Woman Who Cries At Night is too eager to go back home, though. She hasn't said anything, but when I mention it, she gets very quiet,'' Cookie called to him, as Mike walked back toward the 'dobe.

## Chapter Seventeen

*How* *odd*, Mike thought to himself, *that here, of all places, I should run into two Sioux people in such a short period of time. Two of them. So far from home . . . well, that was not right. Jedediah was not so far from home; even though he was half-Sioux. He was home. Home on his own ranch, that his father had left him. Maybe the Apaches wouldn't bother him if they knew he was part Indian, too.*

He reached the door of Toothpick and Mocho's adobe and went inside.

The table where he had left Annie Rose Rushford was empty, but he could hear women's voices coming softly from the back room.

Mocho came out, finally.

She walked over to Mike.

"That woman, she much stubborn. She want to ride to ranch. She say she no care about danger."

Mike shook his head in understanding of Mocho's predicament. She didn't want to be responsible for letting Annie Rushford go out there to her ranch and get killed—or have happen to her what Red Hands—Woman Who Cries At Night—had had happen to her.

"I'll talk to her," Mike said. "I thought she'd agreed to wait."

"Her change her mind plenty fast," Mocho said. "Her try to persuade Jake to take her right now. Jake say 'Wait and see 'til Mike come back.' She mad that Jake not take her right away while you out back with Cookie. She argue but Jake say no. 'Wait for Mike, he say.' "

"Thank you, Mocho."

Mocho shook her head as if perplexed by the woman's stubbornness, and then walked back into the back room.

A minute later, Annie Rose Rushford walked out.

"I suppose Mocho told you that I asked Mr. Herman to take me out to my ranch," she said, as she reached the table where Mike was sitting.

He had sat at the front corner table again, his back to the wall, and looking out at the room. She didn't sit, but stood facing him.

"It sounds like you didn't *ask* so much as insist," Mike said mildly.

"I can take care of myself," she said in a haughty manner.

"Yes. Just like you took care of that cinch," Mike said. He couldn't resist that.

"I don't want your foolishness to get Jake Herman killed. He's a good man."

She didn't answer, but he knew by the look on her face that she was thinking of reminding him of the man she had seen, and probably helped tend to, in the back room.

Wade.

She made her point without saying it.

Suddenly he was sick of waiting around, waiting here

for what—Nat Pierce to ride in? Nat Pierce to have killed Sheriff Rushford in an ambush?

But he wouldn't endanger Jake. Not for this woman. Not for anybody.

"All right, Miss Rushford. If you are so darned set on going to your ranch, *I'll take you!*" he said loudly.

He stood up.

"On one condition. No arguing. If I say 'Go,' you go. If I say 'Stop,' you stop. I don't have time to argue over every little thing with you. For example, I might say, 'Step quietly away from there.' I might see a snake that you don't. By the time you argue about whether or not you *want* to move, the snake could have bitten you.

"If I see an Apache's bright red turban coming toward us, I don't have time to *discuss* it right then in the detail that you seem to like to discuss everything. Please follow my orders at that minute and we can argue about it *later.*"

He stood up, facing her.

She looked him directly in the eye. He looked away first, to indicate that he didn't care whether or not she accepted his offer.

"Those are my terms," he said, crossing his arms in front of his chest and waiting.

Surprisingly, she said, "*Fine!* I'll just get my things." She turned and walked away, going out the door and, he guessed, going over to her horse.

It was only then that it came to him that she'd gotten her own way. He'd been duped.

As he followed her outside, he saw that she had never had her horse unsaddled. She'd merely removed the heavy saddlebags full of items and the large sack of supplies from off the horse.

She was struggling to return the saddlebags onto the

horse when he strode over, took them away from her and put them back on the horse. He put the sack back up.

''Wait here,'' he said.

She mounted her horse as he turned and went inside the adobe building.

He walked over to the curtained doorway and called out.

''Come in,'' Toothpick said.

It had been a long time since Mike had been in the back room; and then he had been in there only a few short times. He tried not to barge in there if he wasn't invited, as it was their private home.

It was still curtained off into three sections; one the main living and cooking area right behind the curtained opening, and the two other rooms behind the curtains that were bedrooms, off to the left.

One curtain was pulled back and Mike could see Wade lying on one of the beds. A large plain brown wooden cross with a carved figure of Jesus on it was directly above Wade's head on the wall at the head of the bed.

Wade's eyes were open just a bit, but Mocho motioned for Mike not to disturb him. She and Toothpick were sitting at a table on the kitchen side of the room. Mike was sure that the curtain was open so that Mocho could keep an eye on Wade.

Mike nodded his head slightly to Mocho to show that he understood. He was happy with what looked like Wade's improvement.

He motioned for Toothpick to come out in the front of the store.

Toothpick got up and followed Mike out into the front room.

''Where's Jake?'' Mike asked.

''Don't rightly know. Over at the stable, I suppose,'' Toothpick said.

"I'm going to take Miss Rushford out to her ranch. We'll be back soon. We'll probably be safe enough, unless Pierce has left a lookout there. Pierce himself is probably somewhere along the trail to Calabasa waitin' to bushwhack Rushford.

Tell Jake . . . no, *ask* Jake, to stay here until I get back. I'll be back as soon as I can."

"Jake might want to come."

"You might need him here, if Pierce comes here. There's people here need protecting," Mike said.

Toothpick didn't need to be told who that was. He knew Mike meant Wade, Red Hands, Mocho, and Cookie, among others. It depended on how much Pierce knew about what was going on.

Everyone at Aguardiente might be in danger, especially if Pierce had found out that it was Toothpick that had sent the marshal's daybook back to Fort Stockton. Pierce was a vengeful man.

Toothpick picked up an empty saddlebag, and began putting some food items inside, as well as some ammunition. Wordlessly, he handed the saddlebag to Mike.

"You might need this," he said.

"Thanks," Mike said. "I think she probably just wants to check on the dog."

"I want to talk to you about something important when you get back," Toothpick said.

"Be back as soon as I can," Mike said.

Outside, he threw the saddlebag on his gelding and mounted up, riding north, following the tracks to the Rushford place for the second time.

Annie Rose Rushford followed silently behind him.

After a while she rode up a little closer and said, "Everything around here is called by a Spanish name," she said, annoyed, and maybe just a little bit condescendingly.

''People call the clay water pots *ollas,*'' she said, ''instead of water jugs.''

She was referring to the large clay pots which hung outside of some of the buildings here in New Mexico. The large clay jugs were filled with water. The breeze kept the water cool.

''They call a herd of horses a *remuda* down here. Ruh-MOO-duh'' she said, pronouncing out the word as if she didn't like it. ''Toothpick says it is Spanish for remount.''

''You need a change of horses—a fresh horse—when you are riding doing ranch work or on the trail with cattle,'' Mike said.

''But why does everything seem to have a Mexican word or a Spanish name for it?''

Dryly, Mike said, ''Well, this is *New* Mexico. New *Mexico* Territory. What did you expect?''

She was silent.

That was good. Thinking was silent, and silent meant not making noise.

Probably she thought he was rude. Not a gentleman. Maybe she was right.

He didn't care what she thought of him, did he?

Anyway, they'd be lucky to get away with their lives intact.

He meant to get her to her ranch, and then get her back to Aguardiente as quick as possible.

They rode for quite a while peaceably, he thought.

Then her period of silence was over.

''You ever think of sheep ranching?''

''No. I'm a *cow*boy,'' he said. He had the cowboy's inherent dislike of sheep; but he didn't want to say so. His Ma wouldn't have liked how blunt and rude he'd been to this woman already.

"You'll need to hire a sheepherder," he said, noncommittally.

"Sheep," she said, on the defensive, "were good enough for the great Kit Carson." They should, therefore, be good enough for *you or any man*."

He knew that it was true that Kit Carson used to have a sheep ranch in Taos, and drove sheep to Sacramento. Carson was a decent man, and well liked and respected. Kit Carson had died in 1868, and Mike had never heard a bad word spoken about him, before or after his death. A good man.

"Sheep and cattle don't get along," he said.

"Oh, pish and poo," she said. "Sheep and cows were together on farms in Europe for . . . well, back to practically the beginning. Mark my words, cows and sheep can exist together."

"I'm a cowboy," he repeated. Was she hinting that he work for her as a sheepherder?

"Always will be," he continued. Get that thought right out of her head immediately, he thought to himself.

"Cows, I'm told," she said primly, sitting up straight in her sidesaddle and looking over at him, "are apt to stampede . . . for rather dumb reasons, I've heard. And they will stampede right off a cliff, I've also heard, and will drown crossing a river."

She tossed her head, her bonnet only stopping the curls on the top half from moving, while the shiny black curls popping out beneath her bonnet bobbed around in emphasis.

"Around here we call them cattle, not cows," he said. "Cows are domesticated. Give milk. These are wild. They're cattle."

She tossed her head, then continued, "All sheep do,

when they're frightened, is huddle closer together. That seems rather a wise thing to do.''

''Sometimes it is, and sometimes it isn't.'' Mike said. Toothpick probably knew of someone she could get to herd her sheep for her; manage her sheep ranch when she went back to Kansas.

He said that.

''I have no intention of returning to Kansas,'' she said, her eyebrows knit together to show her disapproval of what he'd just said.

''I'm staying right here. This is my home now,'' she said.

''Be quiet,'' he said.

''Wha—'' she began to say. Then she shut up.

## Chapter Eighteen

If he remembered right, this was the last rise before her ranch.

He motioned her to wait. He dismounted and began to walk up the rise, intending to look over and inspect the ranch before they went down there.

Instead, he heard the rapid pounding of horse's hoofs behind them. He grabbed his gun out of his holster and turned.

Jake pounded into view, his shiny, big black horse's nostrils flaring with the exertion that he had been put through.

"Shhh!" Annie Rose scolded, as Jake rode up, putting her finger to her lips, much as Mike had seen schoolteachers do when they wanted their students to be still.

Jake dismounted quickly and strode up to Mike.

In deference to what Annie Rushford had just done, Jake spoke in a quiet tone to Mike.

"You didn't think that I'd let you come out here alone, did you?" Jake said. "How come you left me in town?" he said angrily, still keeping his voice low.

"Thought you might be needed there," Mike said.

"I need to be where *you* need me, and that is right here," Jake said. "Toothpick and them can take care of themselves."

There was no sense arguing. It was done. Jake was nothing if not loyal.

"Thanks."

Mike motioned toward the rise. "Just goin' to take a look-see."

Jake joined him, creeping up the back of the rise. There were three horses in sight down below.

They studied the scene.

Neither one had to mention it, but they both realized that more horses might be tied out of sight of the rise, around the other side of the house, which was actually the front.

Dang!

"Pierce's men, all right," Jake said. "Reckonise some of them horses from before."

Jake looked a moment longer.

"Don't see Pierce's horse, though."

"That's because it's under me, fool," a powerful, raspy voice said close behind them.

Some instinctive, gut-level survival sense told them not to whirl around quickly. If they had, they might have been dead instantly and they both knew it.

Mike and Jake turned and stood up slowly at the same time.

Mike's heart began thumping loudly in his chest, as he saw a large man on a horse with a shotgun aimed right at Jake's leather belt buckle, and another, smaller man already dismounted, leading a horse with one hand.

In his other hand, the second man held a shiny silver-and-ivory-handled Colt pointed right at Mike's heart.

Pierce!

Pierce was the one who had spoken with the raspy voice. He was a huge man. He outweighed Mike by a good fifty pounds, and although some of the big gut that was hanging out over his oversize leather belt was fat, a great deal of it was muscle.

His arms and shoulders were huge, and he was a man whose size would strike terror in the heart of any normal-sized jasper in a saloon.

All the features on his large head were oversized; from his nose to his huge mouth. Even his dark brown hair looked overly thick, as if it were too much for his head.

A few weeks had gone by since he'd shaved last, and it gave him a dirty, unkempt appearance, more than it might have on the face of a normal-looking man.

He smelled bad, too.

Poor Red Hands—.

"You look awful familiar," Nathaniel Pierce said to Jake as he casually dismounted. "Ain't I already met you once?"

The two horses stood there as the two outlaws came forward.

Jake didn't answer. He just let his breath out all at once, and Mike could see his chest fall.

"You deef?" Pierce said. It was not a real question, so again, Jake didn't answer. He seemed to not know what to say.

Finally Jake managed a bald-faced lie: "I don't think so. You don't look familiar. I think I'd remember it if I saw you anywhere before."

Keeping his shotgun aimed at Jake's midsection—a warning that Jake would be gut-shot if he made any quick move—Pierce said, "Just walk on up over that hill, the three of you, and on down to that there ranch house. An'

don't plan on givin' me any trouble, as the fewer there are
of you the easier my life gits.''

''You! Over there! Little Lady, git a move on!'' he said
to Annie Rose.

Mike hoped that Annie Rose Rushford had the brains to
keep her mouth shut about who she was; and he hoped that
Pierce didn't know that Bryce Rushford even had a daughter in Kansas.

''Who might you be?'' Pierce asked Annie Rose, as the
group trudged up over the rise and down toward the ranch
house.

''Kate Carson,'' Annie Rose said.

She glanced over at Mike with a smirk on her face.

''Down from Kansas. Came to visit my cousin, here.''
She looked over at Mike. ''He,'' she said, indicating Mike
disdainfully, ''*likes sheep,* and this is supposed to be a
sheep ranch, we heard. So we thought we'd take a ride out.
We were a little surprised to see three horses down there,
because we had heard that only two people lived down
there. I like cattle better, myself. Don't you? So much
smarter than sheep, don't you think?''

Pierce grunted agreement, and gave Mike a look of pure
revulsion and disgust.

''Jake here said that he heard that you were in the area,
so we were looking out for you, Mr. Pierce. Toothpick,
back at Aguardiente, mentioned your name and said that
you were a gentleman. We were looking forward to meet-
ing you.''

She had chattered on so fast that Mike could see that
Nathaniel Pierce was having trouble sorting it all out.
Pierce didn't want to admit it, but he was confused. She
had boondoggled him with her woman's chatter.

For the first time, Mike realized that brutal and vicious
didn't necessarily mean smart.

But that realization didn't make Pierce any less dangerous. In fact, maybe even more so than he had thought before, when he had visualized Pierce as someone smart.

Stupid can be very dangerous.

Unpredictable.

Toothpick had tried to warn him.

Pierce's face was pure ugly. His eyes had none of the
sparkle, that indescribable light inside, that indicated intel-
ligence. Instead there was a dead look in his eyes that gave
the impression that behind those eyes very little thinking
went on.

Mike realized that he was in the most dangerous situation
he had ever faced.

And Jake—death by shotgun—up that close—point-
blank range—was a terrible way to die. Even thinking
about what damage that shotgun would do to Jake . . .

And here was a man—Pierce—who would probably kill
without feeling any emotion; go on and eat a big supper or
have a drink of whiskey ten minutes later with a clear conscience. Or no conscience at all.

Pierce was suspicious, particularly about Jake, but it was
clear that he hadn't quite yet realized where he knew Jake
from.

And Pierce had seemed to sense that there was a compliment in there, somewhere, in what the woman had said.
If he could only figure it out.

Jake wasn't important enough for Pierce's dim brain to
even remember, Mike guessed. At least for now, and until
somebody either jogged his memory or someone down
there at the ranch house remembered Jake.

Pierce either hadn't heard or he was too stupid—or
hadn't figured it out yet—to realize that Jake had given
himself away by attempting to identify the horses down
there.

"Kate" was pretending to be friendly toward Pierce; trying to prolong their lives for as long as she could. She gave Mike no secret looks; she wasn't taking a chance on Pierce detecting her false good cheer.

Mike respected her for that. She had "allied" herself with, even complimented, Pierce, put him in a good mood—and saved all their lives—at least for the moment.

Until they reached the ranch house, which was growing closer with each step.

Mike knew that Jake and Annie Rose were waiting for *him* to do something.

And it was now or never.

Once inside the cabin, they would be outnumbered far more than they were now—this was their best chance; especially since the second man had somewhat relaxed and lowered his Colt off Mike when he saw that the group—especially the woman—seemed to be on somewhat friendly terms with Pierce.

And for some reason, Mike had a gut feeling that the second man was reluctant to be a part of this, to shoot.

But if Mike messed this up, they would all be dead in a few seconds.

First, something caught his eye over near the spring. Something black and white, and wet-looking, lying on the ground. The sight made anger rise up in his gut.

Second, he saw a yellow rock—it might be a chunk of limestone—a few feet ahead of him on his way toward the ranch house—in his path.

As he passed by the rock, he pretended to trip over it.

Already having dismissed Mike as an unimportant, stupid fool because he liked sheep, the men were not particularly threatened by Mike's stumble.

They were ready to say something derogatory, when Mike's arm reached as if to catch himself when he fell. His arm instead slipped smoothly past his holster and his hand came up with his Colt aimed right between Pierce's eyes.

"Drop it. *I said drop it!*" Mike said. His tone of voice left no doubt of what would happen if Pierce didn't comply and soon, before Pierce had a lot of time to think it over.

Jake's own Colt was now out and he was motioning silently with the barrel that the second man was to throw his Colt on the ground also.

Both Pierce and the second man dropped their weapons.

Jake let out a big breath, relieved. Pierce's shotgun was on the ground.

They were not out of the woods yet.

All Pierce had to do was shout and there were probably at least three men who would come running out of the house, guns drawn.

And Jake, Annie Rose, who was unarmed, and himself were standing out here in the open.

Any way he looked at it, they were outnumbered.

He had to move quickly.

"Back over the hill, and no noise out of you or it will be your last!" Mike growled.

He kept his gun on Pierce while Jake kept his gun on the second man.

Annie Rose scurried to pick up Pierce's shotgun and the silver-and-ivory-handled expensive custom Colt the second man had dropped. She was very eager to hurry back up the slight slope and over the rise.

Mike kept his gun on Pierce—who didn't seem to be the least alarmed at the turn of events—in fact he was sneering, as if this was only an unimportant momentary turn of events. Once he tried to edge in close to Mike.

"Back up!" Mike said, almost surprised when Pierce did. This made Mike aware that perhaps Pierce knew something that Mike didn't.

Were more of Pierce's men out here? Somewhere nearby? Why did Pierce treat this as somewhat of a joke? Was it because he thought Mike was nothing but a stupid sheep lover?

"We need to get out of sight," Mike said to Jake and Annie.

But how was he going to work this?

He needed to get all the horses and themselves out of sight, but keep guns on Pierce and the other man until he could get them tied up. How could he do both without leaving one man watching two? That was too dangerous.

Annie was a quick thinker. "You and Jake walk the two men into those trees over there, and let me bring the horses over to you."

It worked.

Mike and Jake escorted the men into the thicket of trees while Annie brought the five horses to the trees where the four men waited.

She held the fancy Colt on the second man while Jake took a rope down off his horse and tied up the two men.

Mike never took his gun off of Pierce's heart.

Knowing his own trick, Jake made sure that he held the rope tight until the men finally had to breathe out and he tied them when their chest was at it's smallest point in the breathing cycle.

"Check them good for knives and other hidden guns," Mike said to Jake.

He did, searching very carefully, in boots, looking for secret places in their clothing for small derringers or other handguns, and knives that might be concealed.

Mike and Jake began trying to put Pierce—not an easy job—it took the two of them—up on Pierce's enormous horse.

It was a kind of horse called a gateado—"gahtay-AHdoh''—around here. It was a dun-colored horse that was striped like a cat. What would Annie Rose say about that when she learned it? If she was going to live here, she'd have to learn a lot of Spanish words like gateado.

''What are you grinning at?'' Annie Rose said.

''Nothing,'' Mike said. He finished heaving the big man up. Pierce adjusted himself on his saddle, his hands tied behind his back.

Pierce made no comment about having to ride with his hands tied behind his back.

The other man had no such qualms, as they put him up in the saddle.

''I'll fall off!'' the second man said. ''You can't do this to me,'' he protested.

Pierce was quiet as Mike and Jake and Annie Rose mounted and began the ride back to Aguardiente.

As they rode, Mike began to realize that perhaps Pierce was right. This was not a good situation. They were going back to Aguardiente. Women were there now that needed protection and there were very few men.

They would be tracked back to Aguardiente and Pierce's men would come to get him.

He wasn't doing Toothpick any good by bringing Pierce to Aguardiente.

What else could he do?

Where the hell was that dang sheriff?

Ironically, Annie Rose and Pierce had something in common: they both didn't like Sheriff Rushford. He wasn't held in high esteem by Toothpick, either.

''We didn't get to feed the dog,'' Annie Rose said regretfully.

''No need,'' Mike replied.

He remembered the black-and-white wet object that he had seen near the spring. Someone had shot the valiant dog.

And stupidly, they had left the dog's body half in and half out of the spring; which would eventually foul the very water that they themselves needed for drinking and cooking.

Stupid. Stupid and cruel.

The smile that lit up Pierce's face was all the answer that Mike needed to know who had done such a thing.

Jake looked at Pierce and then at Mike. Jake was thinking that very same thing. Mike knew by the look in Jake's eyes.

Dang!

There were three levels of vegetation here in New Mexico. In the lower areas, there was cactus, agave, and yucca. A little higher was greasewood and sagebrush. Above that was scrub oak, juniper, and pinyon pine. In some areas, the vegetation overlapped.

This area, on the way back to Aguardiente, was mostly one of cactus, agave, and yucca.

Not much in the way of cover here. And that dang man riding ahead of him on the *gateado* knew it. Pierce was gloating; sure that any minute two bullets would find their mark from a rifle shot from a distance and that Mike and Jake would no longer be any trouble.

What could he do? What could Mike do to cut down chances of that happening?

The woman, he knew, would be saved for something else, some other purpose.

"This will be as easy for my men as slaughtering sheep," Pierce said, confidently, as he spit off to the side of his horse onto a yucca plant.

What did he mean by that?

Mike could only guess.

Pierce's men—having no use for sheep . . . had they used the meek creatures for target practice?

Mike could only guess, but if he had, Mike could only imagine the dog's last moments. He had probably been frantic at the destruction of his flock.

Were the three men inside the ranch house because they had been bitten or tore up?

Mike could only hope so.

*Not that many of us are sure of what their job is in life; but that dog sure did,* Mike thought.

Right now, Mike, Jake, and Annie had a more immediate problem. What should they do? Should they make a run for it to Aguardiente? Or should they look for a place, any slight rise they could hide behind, as Jake would call it— a *trenchera?* And then wait for their pursuers and fight it out?

What should they do?

It was clear by their worried looks in his direction that Annie and Jake were looking for him to decide, to make a decision.

He decided that, for now, they'd keep on going. Every few minutes of time that they were still in their saddles, riding, they were closing the distance between themselves and Aguardiente.

Pierce, of course, was attempting to go as slowly as he could. The last thing he wanted was for Mike and the others to reach Aguardiente, if it could be helped.

He kept attempting to slow his large *gateado* down, and now the second man, catching on, slowed down also.

"Get a move on," Mike said to Pierce.

"Why? Pierce said smugly, "Long Henry, you think we should hurry along like these two varmints say?" He looked over smugly and indicated Mike and Jake, a smirk on his ugly face, completely unworried.

Could the second man be Long Henry McWillie? If it was, he was wanted in Texas for murder. Mike had seen wanted posters for Long Henry as far back as when he worked over in Blue Quail Run.

If it was, Long Henry didn't look a bit like the drawing on his posters. Of course, Long Henry would look a little older now . . . like this man. He remembered something about a special gun on the poster, didn't he?

Sudden realization hit him.

He had *seriously* underestimated the second man with Pierce. No wonder Pierce was chuckling silently to himself.

Long Henry hadn't survived this long by being a fool. This put a bit of a spin on his situation.

Mike had already almost been fooled into thinking that he was unable to ride on his horse with his hands tied behind his back. Long Henry had been playing "helpless." It had almost worked.

Would the gang feel loyalty to Long Henry as well as Pierce?

Maybe so, maybe not.

But what was it? What was it that he knew about McWillie from long ago? Something he knew but had forgotten . . . something else . . .

Annie Rose rode along, oblivious to what Mike was thinking; but Jake had a new, more worried expression that showed that he had picked up on the name.

Jake had never showed fright in his face for as long as Mike had known him, but his expression now was the closest to it that Mike had ever seen.

They had a deadly rattlesnake caught in a delicate silk sack, so to speak, when they should have had a thick burlap bag. Maybe two big rattlers in there.

They rode on.

Mike was more tense than ever.

Annie Rose looked over at him and smiled. A small,

pleasant, genuine smile. She thought things were all right. She had no idea . . .

He didn't smile back.

Her expression changed.

She realized that something was wrong; she just didn't know what. He had no way to tell her.

So far, she had been smart at the way she'd handled Pierce. He was very vulnerable to flattery from a woman. She'd been able to control the situation by her wits, to their advantage.

He didn't want to say anything aloud to change that, in case things went wrong. . . .

Suddenly the picture of the sunburned man—the younger Rushford—sprang vividly into his head.

Tied to the horse . . .

It gave him an idea.

"Pull up for a moment," he said harshly to everyone. He wanted to appear intimidating to Pierce and McWillie. Jake, of course, would not be fooled.

He reined his horse in, and the group stopped.

Neither Pierce nor McWillie had any objections to stopping; they were only too willing.

Jake dismounted and came over. Both he and Mike kept their Colts trained on the two men.

Annie Rose still had the shotgun.

"What if the gang thought that Pierce was dead?" Mike said.

Jake looked at him, not understanding.

"Wouldn't it be a shame if those spyglasses in the distance saw a man slung over his saddle as if he were dead? Would they bother to avenge his death?"

Jake chuckled. "Might if he were a nice guy. Don't know about if he was a no-good sidewinder."

"Now, I don't know if I want to attract attention with a

couple of shots in case there's any other gang members in the area, but a knife fight . . .''

''Can you shoot this if you have to?'' Mike said, looking at the shotgun Annie Rose was holding.

She pointed it in the direction of the two criminals without the least bit of hesitation.

''Yes.'' He had no idea whether or not she was lying.

In an elaborate display, Mike and Jake pulled their knives and pretended to knife McWillie and Pierce, sticking the knives instead in the space between the arms where their elbows bent where their arms were tied behind their backs.

Mike chuckled as he realized that the struggling that the two tied-up men did to thwart this only made the struggle look more realistic.

Afterward, they flung the two ''dead'' men up over their horses, and now Pierce was raging mad; his big stomach bent over the saddle. He tried to kick Mike—he got one fierce kick in—as Mike tied his legs on one side of the horse and his hands together by running additional rope underneath the *gateado's* belly.

Jake did the same with Long Henry McWillie, who, because he was tall and thin, had a less difficult time of it hanging over the saddle.

''Let's git out of here,'' Jake said as he pulled the last bit of rope tight and finished tying it securely.

Pierce raised his head and glared at Annie Rose and Mike knew that her ''grace period'' was over. The look was pure hate, and Mike knew that from now on, if he got the chance, the full brunt of Pierce's cruelty would fall on Annie Rose.

They set off again, and while at first, McWillie and Pierce held their heads up and wiggled defiantly to show they were still alive, after a while, with the horses' hooves plodding along and bouncing, the effort became too great, they grew tired and were forced to ride along as if they truly were dead, their heads hanging and bobbing as the horse trotted along.

Curses and vicious threats flew from Pierce's mouth, while McWillie was silent.

Mike began to realize that perhaps McWillie was a more formidable opponent in that he was a great deal smarter than Pierce, and that McWillie would bide his time and . . .

Still, he personally had no axe to grind with McWillie, and whatever his past back in Texas, he hadn't done anything now that caused Mike to hate him except be in the company of Pierce.

"Sorry, McWillie, I ain't got nothin' personal against you. Mebbee just the company you keep," Mike said. It had come to him what it was—what he remembered about McWillie.

McWillie had been a peaceful medical student; nineteen years old. His best friend was killed in a vicious bank robbery. The robbers had shot his friend first in the arm, and then in the head. His friend had been learning to be a bank cashier.

McWillie had vowed revenge; and had tracked and killed the robbers and fulfilled his promise. The sheriff—now it came back to him—put out a wanted poster on McWillie—was it? Yes, it *was*—a Sheriff Clarence Rushford—now that he thought about it.

McWillie'd brought the money back, but was forced to flee when he found out that *he* himself was now wanted, for the killing of the robbers, of all things.

Gossip was that the robbery was a setup, that the whole thing was set up so that the banker and his cohorts could leave town with the nearby ranchers's money. No one had been able to prove it.

McWillie had gotten a raw deal. In many towns, what McWillie had done would have been considered heroic.

Was this one more indication that Sheriff Rushford was a "bad apple"?

McWillie didn't answer or let on any of what he was thinking. He was smart.

"If it's any comfort, I just remembered who you are. Think you got a raw deal," Mike said.

McWillie was silent; it was clear that he didn't trust anyone in this group.

Mike thought a bit.

"Mind if I ask you just one question?"

McWillie made the effort to raise his head, squinting his eyes, examining Mike for what seemed like a long time. The expression on his face never changed but he said, "I might allow for *one*," McWillie said, his head bobbing. "I ain't got nothin' to lose."

"When did you join up with Pierce, here?"

"Early this mornin'," McWillie said. "Mind if I ask why you're interested in that?"

Pierce raised his head and scowled. "An' brought nothin' but bad luck with him," he said. It was clear that his regard for McWillie had fallen with McWillie's agreement to answer Mike's question.

"McWillie, I think you're a better man than one that needs to have dealings with this man," Mike said, indicating Pierce.

He told McWillie what Pierce had done to the two Rushford men.

"That true?" McWillie asked Pierce.

Pierce shrugged, not answering.

McWillie rode along, silent, his head back down. Mike could see that he was thinking it over, that this news had changed things for him.

"I want Rushford," McWillie said, finally, putting his head back up again. "He was behind the robbery."

He looked over at Pierce.

"But I don't want none of this," he said, indicating Pierce.

Mike took McWillie's gun and threw it in back of a cactus.

Annie Rose and Jake looked over at him questioningly, as they rode, but refrained from saying anything.

Fifteen minutes went by.

Aguardiente was less than five minutes away.

"Pull up," Mike said.

Everyone stopped.

Mike dismounted and motioned to Jake to come and stand near McWillie's horse. He did.

McWillie looked up as Mike spoke to him.

"What's between you and Sheriff Rushford is none of my business," Mike said. "Like I said, I got no quarrel with you. If I let you go, do I have your word that you're through with Pierce here? And will you ride on off away from Pierce?"

McWillie bobbed his head. "Yes. When Pierce sent fer me, I had no idea—thought that we had a lot in common, him bein' after Rushford an' all. Wasn't countin' on him being the way he is—crazy as a bedbug."

Jake looked over at Mike and their eyes met in silent agreement. Annie was silent, but she was watching. It was clear that she had been wondering what they would do with McWillie when they got to Aguardiente.

Jake began to untie McWillie.

"Untie me, too," Pierce said. "I'll jest go away same as him an' no harm done."

"Yer harm has been done already. I'd as soon sleep with a dozen rattlers in my bunk than let you go," Jake said.

"Mike and I saw the results of what you did to the Rush-fords and to our friend Wade."

When he was untied, McWillie slid to the ground. He sat there a minute, rubbing his wrists, then he rose, and swung up on his horse.

Without a backward look, McWillie rode off, back, Mike knew, to pick up his silver-and-ivory-handled gun where Mike had thrown it.

They were safe, at any rate. It would take McWillie half an hour to ride back, get his gun and come after them. If he did.

Mike had a feeling that that would be the last they would see of McWillie.

McWillie had given his word. To a man like McWillie, his word was about all he had left in life. Everything else had been taken away.

Pierce, whose horse was to the right as Mike had talked to McWillie, had been struggling both to get free, and to see what was going on in back of him. His feet were hanging over the side of the saddle toward Mike and Jake.

Now, he gave up and hung down, breathing hard from the effort at straining at his ropes.

He, too, realized that Aguardiente was just five minutes away. He was biding his time. Certain that in Aguardiente, if not now, he would have his chance.

Mike and Jake mounted, and they continued on toward Aguardiente.

Mike looked over at Annie Rose. He had been looking her over since he met her; and he realized that she had been looking him over, also.

But there was something missing. She was a nice lady and all that, and very smart, but he just couldn't get too excited over her.

If the truth be told, he guessed that he still was really thinking about, and still heartbroken over, LuBeth.

LuBeth was so beautiful—and all that he'd ever wanted. But he also knew that even if LuBeth came to him now, and begged him to take her back, that he wouldn't.

As much as he had loved her, he would never again be able to trust her.

Maybe it was just too soon to be looking for another woman. Maybe he just needed more time. But at any rate, he knew that it wouldn't be Annie Rose, much as he had liked her name. Liking her name was not enough.

And he knew, somehow, that Annie Rose had realized that it was not to be, and she would be looking around her for someone else, someone to run her ranch for her, someone else to be husband material. Someone who didn't dislike sheep,

Aguardiente came into sight.

He had to stop thinking about women and worry about the problems at hand, he told himself.

## Chapter Nineteen

They rode up to the adobe. Toothpick and Mocho came outside. Mike, Jake and Annie Rose dismounted without speaking, then Mike and Jake untied Pierce just enough to get him down off the horse.

Mike kept his gun trained on Pierce as Jake retied the rope, making sure that Pierce's hands were tied securely together.

While they were dealing with Pierce, Annie Rose strode past the men without speaking and went quickly past them into Toothpick's place as if she had something to attend to.

Pierce struggled as best he could, but it was no use.

Mike knew that what Pierce had done to Wade was in Jake's thoughts as well as in his own. There was also the brutal slaying of the marshal and what Pierce had done to the two Rushford men. And to Red Hands.

This man had affected all of them, in one way or another. How could one man be so evil?

And what about Sheriff Rushford? Where was he? What good was he if he had done what people seemed to think he had done? How could he turn Pierce over to Sheriff Rushford in all good faith?

More than anything, more than McWillie's opinion, it was Annie Rose's face when Sheriff Rushford was first mentioned that made him wonder—.

First things first.

"What are we going to do with Pierce now?" Toothpick said. Jake, Mocho, and even Pierce were all looking at him.

As if he had the answer.

He didn't.

He did know one thing. When you're discouraged, that's when you gotta show courage—and keep going.

The possibilities were: Toothpick's place, the livery, and the wickiup.

The wickiup—no—Red Hands would have a knife in him before you could say "skedaddle."

But it wasn't fair that Toothpick's place be attacked and take the brunt of it if Pierce's men arrived.

What, then? What should he do?

They were all standing around silently watching him; waiting for *him* to come up with the answer of what to do. *Him,* Footloose. Of all people.

The livery stable? Should he ask a one-armed man, who probably already had had enough troubles in life to get dragged into this?

That didn't seem fair either.

His uncle would have said that Mike was "on the horns of a dilemma."

He could see only one solution.

"When is Sheriff Rushford due to get here?" he asked Toothpick.

"Tomorrow, late, probably." Toothpick said.

"I'm going to take Pierce and ride out and camp overnight a mile or two outside of town. Late tomorrow I'll bring him back here.''

It was the only thing he could think of.

''Jake can stay here with the rest of you to give you protection in case Pierce's men come here.''

Toothpick nodded.

With Jake, even if Pierce's gang rode in, they would have enough men and guns to hold them off until the sheriff arrived.

Mike assumed that the sheriff was not coming alone.

''I'll have Mocho get you a sack of provisions,'' Toothpick said.

''No need. I still have what you gave me earlier. Jake will tell you what happened after I leave,'' Mike said to Toothpick.

They sat Pierce on the wooden sidewalk outside the store, and Toothpick went inside.

Mike went to the *olla*—the large water jug—hanging in the shade of the porch roof and filled up three canteens, his own, the one Jake handed him off Jake's own horse, and the one from Pierce's horse.

''You sure you want me to stay here?'' Jake asked.

''Don't worry, Pierce will be trussed up like a Christmas goose the whole time,'' Mike said. Toothpick came back out.

''Shoot the jasper 'tween the eyes if he gives you any trouble,'' Toothpick said, looking directly at Pierce.

Pierce narrowed his eyes and spat on the ground, but he stayed silent as he looked evilly at Toothpick.

In a way, that was scarier than if he yelled or spoke back to Toothpick. At least then, Mike would have known that Pierce was scared.

This way, it was more of a mystery what Pierce knew or planned.

Mike knew one thing: He was not looking forward to spending a night out there alone with this rattlesnake of a man.

He knew one thing: He couldn't wait to turn over this man to Sheriff Rushford. Maybe they deserved each other. And he was curious to meet this man, Sheriff Rushford, who so many people had expressed so many opinions about: Toothpick, Annie Rose, and McWillie.

A lawman no one seemed to have one good word to say about.

Dang!

# Chapter Twenty

Mike rode out of Aguardiente with Pierce. They rode about two miles out, heading eastward, and then Mike began looking for a place—a *trenchera*—where they could hide out until late the next day.

It was still very hot.

There was nothing in this mostly flat, desert scrub area that provided much cover, and finally Mike realized that he would have to settle for a scrub-covered hollow.

Toothpick had included a coffeepot but Mike had decided on a cold camp—there would be no fire tonight.

Pierce, when he figured that out, let loose a barrage of oaths.

Mike ignored him.

Just before dusk, he gave Pierce a drink of water and some biscuits and ham that Toothpick had wrapped in a cloth in the sack. Pierce ate it with his hands tied tight in front of him.

The sunset was one of those which had incredibly beautiful pink and purple clouds very high up which made Mike

166

hate to see the big red-orange ball behind them go down. He wished this sunset—all that incredible beauty—would last for a longer time, but the sun was sliding quickly down below the horizon much too fast.

No rain clouds in sight, he thought, as he checked the area around Pierce for rocks that could be used to bash Mike in the head, in the night. He threw all the rocks that looked like good head-bashing ones far off into the short, desert shrubbery.

He tied Pierce's legs together for the night.

Judging from that sunset, tomorrow would be another hot day. In the morning, he would see about rigging a blanket on something to provide some protection from the sun.

But that was tomorrow.

In a minute, he'd eat a few bites of his own ham and biscuit and throw a blanket over the bitter-looking, very large, angry man five feet away from him.

He'd shake the blanket that he had removed from Pierce's horse very well to be sure that nothing was concealed in it before he gave it to him.

Tonight, he wouldn't be getting any sleep. That was all right. He'd gone without sleep before, when on the trail with a herd, especially when there was trouble. That was part of his foreman's job.

If he fell asleep tonight, Pierce would be gone in the shrubbery in a flash. Even though he was tied, he would crawl if he could.

It was the last few minutes of light left; the last glow of light left from the sun which had slid now below the horizon.

It would be a long night, Mike thought, as he poured water from the second canteen into his black hat to give both horses a drink, keeping his eye on Pierce at the same time.

The poor gelding. It had been kind of hectic lately. He was like family to Mike. And he'd been being sadly neglected. He hadn't had oats since his stay in the livery stable that day. Mike promised himself that he'd get some oats for Browny as soon as he could, tomorrow evening.

Speaking of family, he worried a little about money . . . he had to get a job soon so he could send money to Austin.

He'd used up quite a bit of his money for food; first paying Cookie back for his share of the food that Cookie'd brought, then at Toothpick's place, and he still had to settle up at the livery stable, and he'd given a little money to Hawk in that blue bandanna.

He went back and took care of Pierce. Pierce accepted the blanket silently, giving Mike a look of pure hate.

Mike hoped that this whole mess would be over soon.

Maybe tomorrow, he thought, as he looked over one last time where the horses were picketed in the same hollow behind him, silently checking them before he sat down again about eight feet away from Pierce.

It was getting dark.

Surprisingly, Pierce snored loudly most of the night, deep rumbling snores . . . sleeping like someone without a care in the world, while Mike strained his eyes in the darkness, until the moon came up, to be sure that Pierce made no sudden or slowly creeping move to attack him in the dark.

As usual, the clear deep blue-black desert night sky sucked up the heat of the day quickly and the night grew cold. Mike was glad to have his blanket.

Pierce's loud snores would have kept him awake anyway, even if they were the best of friends and he was trying to sleep, he thought to himself about three in the morning.

Dawn seemed to take forever, as it always seemed to when you want it to arrive in a hurry, Mike thought.

All Mike wanted was for this day to be through quickly.

He gave the horses a drink and was surprised to find some oats that Toothpick had included in the very bottom of the sack. He gave some to each horse.

Pierce was still snoring.

The horses were lucky because they were picketed where there was a small patch of grass. It was a low patch and water must collect there sometimes after the rain.

When Pierce awoke, Mike gave him some more biscuits and ham. Pierce made a face, but took the food and drank the water that Mike gave him in a tin cup.

Right after that, Mike took his own blanket and, finding two shrubs a short distance apart, he rigged the blanket as a kind of a lean-to with some rope. He made the opening face west, as the sun rose in the east.

He and Pierce went inside, as far back out of the sun as they could as the sun rose and it grew hotter and hotter all morning.

Things were quiet in the intense heat until mid-afternoon, when a desperate-looking Mexican man crawled out of the shrubs facing Mike and Pierce.

"Agua . . . agua," the man said, his face barely an inch above the dirt, facing down, as he crawled toward them—his large black-and-silver Mexican-looking sombrero almost all that Mike could see of the man as he crawled slowly out of the bushes toward them.

The Mexican was crying for water.

"Agua," the man said once again—faintly—as if to say it again was almost too much for him. Then he collapsed, flat on the ground.

It looked as if he had passed out.

The Mexican's old black shirt and well-worn black trousers were all covered with dust, as if the man had crawled a long way.

Mike got up and went toward the man, his gun out and

ready. When he reached the man, he went to help him up. The man sprang up and knocked the gun out of Mike's hand.

"You!" Mike said.

"You!" the man answered back as a wisecracking joke.

It was no joke.

He had a well-used Colt pointing at Mike's gut.

It was Rusty. The man from Aguardiente. The man that the two women had been fighting over.

Mabel and Alice. Alice Fickerby. The woman who had bought the chickens.

In a flash, Mike realized that it all fit.

Pierce's nonchalance about being caught.

Mike's gut feeling that there had to be a closer hideout than the one that Jake and Wade had been taken to.

The wagonload with so many supplies that Rusty and Mabel had bought. Much more than two people needed.

And if Rusty rode in to Aguardiente, there was no reason why he would not be told what was happening; because Toothpick and the rest would think that Rusty would be *helpful* and on their side.

All Rusty had to do was circle around until he came upon Mike and Pierce.

And Mike had a glimpse—a deadly glimpse—of how good an actor Rusty was, and how that might explain why so many men had been disappearing around Aguardiente; coming and going.

And why Rusty had so many twenty-dollar double eagles to spend on supplies when he apparently didn't do much work on his ranch.

Mike only had seconds to run this through his head. His gut instinct was to act fast before he had a bullet in his gut.

It was now or never. In seconds, he could be dead. In

seconds, Rusty could raise the gun and shoot him through the head.

Following a gut instinct, he rushed forward, as surprised almost as Rusty, and they crashed to the ground and rolled together in the dust.

He was lucky enough to shove the pistol off to the side so that Rusty's first shot went off harmlessly into the brush.

They rolled to the left and Mike was on the other side when Rusty rolled into the spines of an agave as Rusty shot again.

Each agave leaf—jutting out from the plant's circle like shape—had a sharp spine on the end, and Rusty let out an equally sharp yell.

Mike couldn't help being glad. That was a very dirty trick Rusty had played in an area where a man dying of thirst was a serious thing. Mike was angry. Used Mike's compassion to play him for a sucker.

With a strong thrust, Rusty angrily pushed back, rolling toward Mike.

Pierce, as best as he could see, was sitting watching, still in the lean-to, confident that Rusty—who weighed forty or fifty pounds or so more than Mike—would have no trouble beating Mike to a pulp and then killing him.

In fact, Pierce had a look of glee on his face.

Mike and Rusty scrambled quickly to their feet at the same time, and Rusty came at Mike again trying to aim the pistol at him for the third shot.

Mike grabbed Rusty's right wrist, which was holding the pistol, and twisted it as hard as he had ever twisted anything in his life.

Maybe the years of roping and branding cattle helped him. Mike never knew. But he managed to twist Rusty's arm and hand until the gun slipped out of Rusty's huge fingers and fell to the dirt between them.

In a flash, Mike was down and up and Rusty's gun was in Mike's hand now.

"Get yer hands over your head! Now!" Mike said forcefully, fully prepared for the consequences if Rusty didn't comply—and Rusty knew it. He must have read it in Mike's eyes.

Both Pierce and Rusty looked surprised.

It had never occurred to them, it seemed, that this would be the outcome.

"You stupid fool!" Pierce said, looking up at Rusty from inside the crude lean-to shelter. "You got to pertend to be dyin' of thirst! You always like to do that! You shoulda just shot him in the back from out in the bushes like I woulda done."

He shook his head in disgust. "What a fool! Now look at the mess you got us both in."

"I got us both in!"

"Yes, you! I shoulda never trusted this job to one of my dang stupid cousins! You shoulda just bushwhacked 'em!"

Rusty replied, "You liked yer share of the money well enough, Nat!"

Rusty went to lunge at Pierce, but Mike pushed the Colt into Rusty's back jamming the barrel of the pistol, hard, against Rusty's wide back right over the section where it would shoot right into Rusty's heart, reminding Rusty to stay put.

But it wasn't over yet.

It was a desperate situation.

If Mike went to get rope, he could not keep the gun on Rusty. Unfortunately, the gelding was picketed so that Mike couldn't whistle for him.

There was only one way he could think of to do this. He was already behind Rusty, since Rusty had turned to lunge at Pierce, so he turned the pistol quickly and buffaloed him—he used the handle of Rusty's own gun to knock Rusty out.

Rusty slid to the ground—out cold.

Mike hurried to get a rope and tied the big man up tight, before he came to, stopping on his way to pick up his own Colt from the dirt.

A few minutes later, he watched Rusty come to, and shortly after that, Mike decided he'd had enough of this dang campout.

He got his two prisoners mounted up, finding Rusty's horse a short distance away.

He untied their legs so they could mount, then retying them beneath each horse's belly, as insurance.

Then the three of them headed back to Aguardiente.

## Chapter Twenty-one

$A$s Mike rode into sight of Aguardiente, he was relieved to see a tumbleweed wagon in front of Toothpick and Mocho's adobe.

A tumbleweed wagon was a traveling jail cell—used to transport prisoners in isolated areas to court.

Marshals tended to use them more than sheriffs, but Mike didn't care who had it or whose it was—he was more than happy to see it there.

Three unsavory-looking men were already in the tumbleweed wagon; and he guessed that Sheriff Rushford had been out to the Rushford place on his way here and had made a clean sweep of the rest of Pierce's gang.

No, there were four men in the wagon.

One more man had his back turned and was facing the corner. Mike couldn't get a good look at him.

On his way by, he looked carefully and yes, sure enough, it looked like the three clumped together in the middle of the wagon had a few dog bites, their clothing ripped and

174

torn a bit as if they had been in a scuffle with something owning sharp teeth. Dog teeth, Mike hoped.

He knew he was right about the three men when Rusty and Nathaniel Pierce started cursing when they saw the three men inside the tumbleweed wagon.

Up till then, they had not been too upset at being brought into Aguardiente as prisoners, figuring that the three gang members out at the Rushford place would come into town and rescue them.

This turn of events upset the outlaw cousins. They started cursing and blaming each other.

Hearing the horses's hoofbeats, Toothpick came to the door. A smile spread slowly across his lips as he saw Pierce still tied up, and a questioning look followed as he looked at Rusty, then at Mike, for an explanation.

Mike told what had happened, about Rusty pretending to be a Mexican needing water, and about coming to try to free Pierce.

Mabel heard.

Mabel pushed past Toothpick, almost knocking him over as he stood in the doorway. Putting her hands angrily on her hips, she came out onto the plank porch and scolded Rusty loudly, as Mike dismounted and tied the three horses to the hitching post.

"Dang it, Rusty Cuthbert! What kind of trouble you got yerself into now! You promised me! You promised me you were through with trouble—and with *him*," she said, looking at Pierce angrily. "You been sneakin' food out to the shack behind our place for these outlaws? You made an outlaw hideout out of our spread?"

His not answering was her answer.

For the first time, Mike had heard Rusty's last name: Cuthbert.

Her anger turned to tears.

Rusty didn't want to look her in the eye. He turned away. There were too many witnesses for him to talk nicely to her, to say he was sorry.

Seemingly out of nowhere, a small crowd was gathering. There were more people than Mike had ever seen in Aguardiente.

Almost everyone Mike knew was there; including Jake, Cookie, Red Hands, Mocho, Ted Buchanan, and about five other men Mike didn't know. They were all listening. Three of the men watching had tin badges on their shirts.

Mabel didn't care; her life was now in ruins in front of her eyes.

"I wondered," she said, "where you been gettin' all that money lately . . . Oh, Rusty, how could you?" the woman's anger had turned to tears.

"I should have known," she said, sadly, tears creeping slowly down her cheeks as she stood on the plank sidewalk. She turned slowly and went toward the doorway, as if the sight of Rusty tied up was too much for her to bear.

"He *promised*," she said fiercely, mostly to herself.

Mike felt sorry for Mabel. What would she do now?

"Why did I believe that story he tole about sellin' those scrawny beeves for so much money?" she said to herself as she pushed past Toothpick to go back inside. It was clearly a question that she expected no one to answer. Her head hung down on her chest as if she had been shamed. She stood behind Toothpick in the doorway.

Clearly she was telling herself the same thing that Mike had said to himself only a few days ago. *If he loved me, he wouldn't have done what he did.* Just as Mike had said to himself about LuBeth: *if she loved me, she wouldn't have done what she did.*

She took one last look at Rusty and then disappeared

into the darkness inside, probably to cry. Toothpick left the doorway, probably to comfort Mabel.

Mike was surprised as he looked at the empty doorway to see Wade now standing there.

He grinned at Mike in triumph, as if to say, "Look at me, I'm better—I'm standing up."

On Wade's head was a big clean white bandage. As he stood there, Annie Rose's head slid under Wade's armpit, as if to help steady him. Her right hand appeared around his waist on the other side as she stood close. She smiled up at Wade.

Mike grinned.

Annie Rose had obviously found "her new man." The man she was looking for. A good choice, he felt like telling her. A good steady man. One who *might* not hate sheep.

And if Wade hated sheep, Mike had the feeling that Annie Rose might not mind raising a few cattle on that ranch. Mike had a feeling that all her sheep were dead, anyway— slaughtered for sport by Rusty, Pierce, and the three men in the tumbleweed wagon.

In that case, Wade and Annie Rose could start over with cattle or pigs, or whatever they chose.

He'd have to speak to Wade about cleaning out and improving that spring at the ranch—no, Wade would know enough to do that himself.

Wade and Annie Rose stepped aside to let Toothpick out of the doorway.

As Mike looked over at Toothpick, he remembered that he hadn't congratulated Toothpick on his book getting published. He'd have to do that.

Mike walked over to Toothpick.

A man came out of Ted Buchanan's livery stable and walked toward them. Medium height, thin but muscular, he had two tied-down ivory-handled guns and looked as if he was confident using them. He had on a hat the color of desert sand, sandy colored hair and a light brown shirt and jeans. Good brown boots. Brown leather belt and holsters. A man whose clothing would make him hard to spot in the desert.

Mike's impression was that the man was a decent, law-abiding man of strength and wisdom. There was something about his manner that gave that impression.

"That's the deputy that came with the sheriff," Toothpick said to Mike.

The deputy came over and took a moment to size up Mike, and look over Pierce and Rusty—still in their saddles, their horses tied to the hitching post, before he spoke. He seemed to approve of what he saw, too.

"That Nathaniel J. Pierce?" he said to Mike.

Mike nodded.

"Mr. Pierce, we been lookin' for you somethin' fierce," he joked. "I'm James Longley." He looked at the other man, then at Mike. "And who might this other *gentleman* be?" It was clear James Longley had a sense of humor.

A few people snickered at the word gentleman.

"Rusty is a cousin of Nathaniel," Mike said.

The deputy raised his eyebrows. "I'm assuming that he's not tied up on account of attending church too often, so I'm assuming that he's one of the Pierce gang."

Mike nodded.

"I'll want to be talking to you in a few minutes in some detail," he said to Mike. "I'll need to take your statement."

The three men with badges came forward to get Rusty and Nathaniel Pierce off their horses. Cookie and Jake stood ready to help or draw their guns if need be.

Mike breathed a sigh of relief as he watched the deputy

help padlock the two outlaws in the tumbleweed wagon, in the closest seats to the back, where the door was.

''Where's Sheriff Rushford?'' Mike asked Deputy Longley as the deputy turned and indicated that Mike follow him inside Toothpick's store.

Longley stood there while he answered Mike's question.

''He won't be of much use to you,'' Longley said, and Mike had a feeling that Longley would be shedding no tears over that fact. ''Matter of fact, he's the fourth man in the tumbleweed wagon—that one, back there in the far corner with his back to us, hiding his face in shame.''

With this, Pierce let out a yell, and tried to fight and kick his way towards the place where Sheriff Rushford was sitting. He succeeded only in getting himself tied to the bars nearest where he had been sitting by two of the men with badges on.

The men appeared very capable.

Pierce was sweating, spitting, and yelling in outrage.

None of this seemed to bother James Longley.

''Sheriffs . . . well, they can go bad, just like anyone else, I suppose, but it sure is a sorry thing when they do,'' James Longley said. ''Seems Rushford had a bank robbery scheme whereby he robbed a bank and then split the bank money with the bankers. Was pulling this same scheme up a day's ride out of Calabasa, and this time, he was unlucky enough to get caught. Lord knows how many times he has pulled this scheme before.

''The poor townspeople who had their money in the bank were the ones who'd take the loss.''

Longley shook his head in disgust and then added, ''We got a tip ahead of time and I was up there waiting for him when he tried to pull it off. I got the message to come here next. So here I am.''

Mike nodded. ''I think he did pull this same thing before.

There's a man named McWillie—Long John McWillie—
that I think that you ought to talk to,'' Mike said. ''Pulled
that same thing in Texas once. McWillie got the blame. I
know McWillie would like to get his name cleared.''

''I might just do that,'' James Longley said. ''Thanks for
the tip. Think I might have heard something about that.''

Longley turned and looked over at Jake in a friendly
manner.

''Jake here's been fillin' my ears since I got here. Tole
me the whole story, from the beginning. Gave me directions to the other hideout, in the canyon. I'll be takin' a
ride up there, soon's I get enough men together. See if
there's any gang members left. Need to clean out the whole
nest of 'em.

''Talked some to Toothpick, here, too. I'll need to check
around and see if anyone else has gone missing in the surrounding area.''

After he said that, the deputy turned and went inside.

Before he followed, Mike looked over at Red Hands—
Woman Who Cries At Night. It looked like maybe her
hands would remain the same color they were now.

She was glaring at Pierce, but it was clear from the puzzled blank look in his eyes as he looked back at her that
Pierce didn't even remember her.

Mike walked over to Red Hands. ''Let the Deputy take
care of him, Woman Who Cries At Night.''

She didn't say yes or no. The expression on her face was
unreadable. But the truth was that it was out of her hands,
unless she wanted to trail the tumbleweed wagon back to
court.

Which she might.

In which case, they'd better have a close guard around
the tumbleweed wagon at night or they might get an un-
pleasant surprise in the morning, courtesy of her knife.

Mike's hope was that Cookie, now, maybe was more important to her. Cookie slid his hand into hers; interlocking their fingers gently. Maybe her life with Cookie was more important to her now. Only time would tell, and only Woman Who Cries At Night knew for sure.

Maybe she would, could choose a new name for herself now . . . or maybe soon.

Mike thought that probably Pierce would end up being hung, in Calabasa, for one crime or another. Then maybe the Sioux woman's quest would finally end.

When the U.S. marshal got here from Texas, he would probably go to the court at Calabasa to add his two cents' worth. One way or another, Nathaniel Pierce's goose was finally cooked. He would be hung for one or another of his murders.

Mike's guess was that a similar fate might be waiting for Rusty when James Longley investigated further.

Mike went inside and joined the deputy at the same table where Mike had sat when he first arrived at Aguardiente.

Toothpick and Jake came over to the table, and sat down with the deputy and Mike.

The deputy asked Mike a few questions, then he got up and left to go outside, saying, "I'll need to talk to you again in a few minutes, Mr. Conroy. I have to speak to my men."

Toothpick said, "I wanted to talk to you, too. Things have been movin' so fast around here that I haven't had a chance. But this place is growing. I'm going to start building two more 'dobes, right next to this building, one and then t'other. One will be a saloon, and the other a restaurant.

"This here 'dobe, I'm goin' to leave be the store. Pretty soon this place is goin' to be a real live town. I was wonderin' if you and Jake are plannin' to stick around. I got lots of jobs for you. There'll be the saloon to run, and the restaurant . . .''

Mike shook his head. "Can't rightly see myself tied down runnin' a saloon or a restaurant. I'm a cowpoke."

"What about being the town marshal here?"

"No, I don't think I'm cut out for the law, neither." Mike thought about the nights out in the open when the cattle were quiet, or softly lowing, and the blue-black sky was filled with sparkling white dots . . . millions of stars, and he realized just where he was the happiest.

Maybe he'd forget the ladies for a while until he got his life straightened out.

"Mabel will be needin' a job," he said to Toothpick, "and so might Wade and Annie Rose, for money to restock their ranch, and maybe Cookie and Woman Who Cries At Night."

He meant to speak to Cookie and Woman Who Cries At Night to ask them if they might consider taking a ride over to that lonely boy's ranch—Jedediah Jones's ranch—and see if he wanted to hire some help. He'd tell them to say that Mike Conroy had sent them.

He had a feeling that Cookie, Woman Who Cries At Night, and Jedediah Jones would all get along real fine. Make a right nice family.

He told that to Toothpick, and remembered to congratulate Toothpick on his book that was being published.

Then Mike said, "I'll follow the tumbleweed wagon to Calabasa, with Jake and whoever else wants to come along and testify against Pierce, but then I think that Jake and I . . . unless Jake is interested in one of the openings you have for a job . . .''

Mike and Toothpick looked over at Jake.

Jake just shook his head, so Mike continued, "I think maybe Jake and I will be ridin' down El Paso way."

He looked at Jake.

"Think that sounds like somethin' you'd like to do, Jake? Ride down to El Paso and take a look at that ranch you tole me about?"

"Sounds like a good idea to me," Jake said smiling. "Sounds like a *dang* good idea."